Patricia David r[...]
is cheap chocola[...]

She nodded gri[...]

Erthmun straightened a little, though he was still bent over the body. It was naked and it had been hacked up so completely that blood covered it like a body stocking. Even the long hair was covered with it. Its natural colour may have been blonde, Erthmun thought, but he couldn't be sure. The pretty, oval face, however, looked as if it had been meticulously cleaned and the pale skin here, contrasted with the nearly total covering of blood on the body and hair, was jarring.

Erthmun said, to no one in particular, 'She looks like a mime, a mime.' He bent over the body again and stared into its open eyes, which were bright jade green. 'Beautiful,' he said. 'I don't think I've ever seen eyes quite this colour before.'

'Those are contacts,' Patricia told him.

He glanced quickly at her. 'Are they?' he said. Patricia thought for a moment that Erthmun was toying with her, although that would have been unlike him. She knew, for him, humour was not a necessity of everyday living.

Also by T. M. Wright in Gollancz Horror

T.M.
WRIGHT
ERTHMUN

GOLLANCZ HORROR

First published in Great Britain 1995
by Victor Gollancz
An imprint of the Cassell Group
Wellington House, 125 Strand, London WC2R 0BB

A Gollancz Horror paperback original

© T. M. Wright 1995

The right of T. M. Wright to be identified as
author of this work has been asserted by him
in accordance with the Copyright, Designs
and Patents Act, 1988.

A catalogue record for this book is
available from the British Library.

ISBN 0 575 05872 2

Typeset by CentraCet Ltd, Cambridge
Printed and bound in Great Britain
by Cox & Wyman Ltd, Reading, Berks

Again,
this book is for Cindy,
with love

The House on
Four Mile Creek

Prologue

The creature's big sky-blue eyes followed the long, slowly merging vertical lines and the contours of the great buildings around her. The lines undulated, as if she were seeing merely some reflection on slowly moving water. She recognized the buildings. She recognized the city. It was a black splotch on her memory. It smelled bad, and the air moved leadenly about in her lungs, as if it might solidify.

It was a place of death. Not the kind of death that serves and nourishes the earth, but the kind that is sudden and needless, the kind that leaves behind it a heavy and sweltering grief – an emotion that the creature had felt in others more than once, and had found confusing.

There were a thousand similar places on the earth, the places that the others called home. Places which, before the buildings had been put up to cut the sky apart, and before the subways sliced through the earth, and before the dark blanket of streets and parking lots smothered the soil, had been the place of their birth. The places where they had first sprung up. The places which had nourished them, and given them pleasure. And then had watched them die. And spring up again. And die.

The places which, at last, men had found and driven them from and claimed for their own. The places which men had changed into something foul, something that hurt under foot, and assaulted the ears, and had a strange, harsh, unliving pulse of its own.

Approximately one-and-a-half million people live on the island of Manhattan. It's shaped roughly like a heel-less shoe, viewed from above, with the ankle at its northern end, and it covers about thirty-one square miles, eight of which are inland waterways.

Manhattan is the smallest of New York City's five boroughs – Queens, Brooklyn, Manhattan, The Bronx, and Staten Island. Several ethnic and cultural areas have sprung up on the island, including – looking south to north – Chinatown, near the island's southern tip, Greenwich Village, about a mile north, Stuyvesant, a half-mile east of Greenwich Village, and, a mile and a half northwest, the Garment District, then the Theater District.

East of Central Park, there is the Upper East Side, and Yorkville. Northwest of Central Park, there is

Morningside Heights, home of Columbia University.
And east of Morningside Heights, Harlem. East of
Harlem is East Harlem.

The Harlem river cuts the island off from land at its
northern end. On the west, it is separated from land
by the Hudson river, and on the east by the East river.
Upper New York Bay is at its southern end.

Peter Minuet purchased the island from the Manhattan Indians in 1624. He paid twenty-eight dollars.

A first-time visitor to the island is struck by the very
pace of things. Business is the business of Manhattan,
and it is accomplished with all possible speed. If you
are walking, you walk fast, with your head down,
and you talk to no one. If you are driving, you drive
fast and, of necessity, view the other drivers with a
cool, if not always quiet, disdain. The rule of thumb
that applies in Manhattan – both to pedestrians and
drivers alike – is: if you get there first, you have the
right of way.

The first-time visitor to Manhattan is also struck by
the attitude of New Yorkers. Publicly, it is a thin-
lipped, stiff-legged stoicism that says very loudly, *I'm
minding my own business, you mind yours. If you want to
run around naked, for Christ's sake, it's okay with me, as
long as you don't invade my space*. It is an attitude that
first-time visitors often mistake for discourtesy. It
isn't. It's survival. In a city the size and complexity of
Manhattan, no one can afford to mind anyone's
business but his own.

The first-time visitor is also struck by the order of things. The drivers drive like maniacs, yes, and the pedestrians aren't much better, and there's nothing but foul air to breathe, thousands of miles of pavement, millions of square yards of buildings to look at, and a constant din of cars, and people ... But everything looks as if it's pre-ordained. Everything seems to work. There is order to the chaos. For some first-time visitors, it is a very, very disconcerting experience. There can't *be* such order in a place like this. It's not natural. But, of course, there has to be order in a place like this because, if there wasn't, it would fall apart.

One

Erthmun remembered being left alone in a cave when he was a child. He maintained that he was less than a year old when this happened, although everyone else in his large family told him that that was pure fantasy. Some of them even laughed, which Erthmun thought bordered on cruelty because childhood memories were sacred, after all. Childhood itself was sacred. Adulthood wasn't. Adulthood was profane, violent and perverse. Erthmun often wondered why nature allowed human beings to grow beyond the purity of childhood.

He remembered that, as a child, he had owned pets. This was pure fantasy, too, according to the other members of his family. They reminded him that Erthmun's father had harboured no particular fondness for animals, and was – according to family legend – not above shooting stray cats and dogs that happened onto the family property.

The cave that Erthmun remembered was small and dark, and it smelled of newly mown grass. This memory was particularly strong for him, as memories of smells are for everyone. It haunted his nights and clouded his days, though not all of his nights, or all of his days.

'Do you remember if you were alone in the cave?' his sister Lila once asked.

'Alone in the cave,' Erthmun said. It was not a question: he was repeating what she had said.

'Yes,' said his sister, and grinned.

'Yes,' Erthmun said.

'You were?' his sister said, still smiling. 'Alone in the cave, I mean.'

'I was alone,' Erthmun said. 'Yes.'

'You know, of course,' she told him, 'that this memory is something you've concocted to take the place of another memory. One that's probably even worse.'

Erthmun nodded. 'Even worse,' he said.

'Jack,' his sister told him, 'it's a widely accepted concept.' She smiled again, though Erthmun could not imagine, at the time, why she was doing so much smiling. She finished, 'Manufactured memories to take the place of other memories. It's a widely accepted concept.'

'A widely accepted concept,' Erthmun said, and when she smiled yet again, he wanted suddenly to bash her head against a wall. The impulse came and went as quickly as a twitch; he found it very confusing

– though it was far from the first time that such an impulse had come to him – and he was ashamed of himself.

Erthmun did not often see his family; his two sisters lived within an easy commute from Manhattan, and his mother lived in a comfortable home in White Plains, also an easy commute. He got along with his sisters, and his mother, when he saw them on holidays – Christmas, Thanksgiving – when people are required to get along, because, according to social convention, these are times when people should.

The man that Erthmun had known as his father died when Erthmun was five years old. This had been the impetus for his mother to pack up their belongings and move him and his sisters out of their house on Four Mile Creek, in the Adirondacks (the house in which Erthmun was born). It was a move she had been wanting desperately to make for a long time, but one that Erthmun's authoritarian father had nixed because the house on Four Mile Creek was, as he put it, 'safely removed from the muck and mire and moral decay of the cities'.

Erthmun did not remember much about his father. He remembered only that there were many times that he saw himself in his mind's eye stealing into his parents' bedroom late at night, or stealing into his father's study while the man read, or stealing up behind him while the man sprayed weed-killer on his little, mannered garden, and reaching into the man's

back and tearing his spine out, and then running
through the fields with it, the spine held high over
his head, as if it were a great and dangerous snake,
and he had defeated it in battle.

Erthmun did not feel connected to his sisters or his
mother. They sensed this, and it confused them. His
sister, Sylvia, once told him, 'Molasses is thick, Jack,
but blood is thicker, and if you ask me, families
should be as thick as thieves.'

'Thick as thieves,' Erthmun said, though he had
not understood it. The whole concept of families
seemed odd to him. He could sense how his sister felt
when she talked about families; he sensed much. But
he did not get the same sort of warm and fuzzy
feelings that she got when she talked about families,
and he told her so.

'You're a strange duck,' she said.

'I'm not a duck at all,' he said, and though she
cracked a smile, she hid it, because she knew that
Erthmun was being entirely serious.

Erthmun's impulses to violence were quick, but
rarely acted upon. His own reflection – in a mirror, in
a pond, in the polished metal surface of a car – often
made his muscles tense and his hands ball up into
fists. He had once hit a bathroom mirror with his fist,
in response to seeing his reflection. It made him feel
foolish because, when he thought about it, he could
think of no good reason for hitting the mirror. His
reflection had ... excited him, angered him. As if
what he was seeing in the mirror had been a stranger,

and an enemy, not merely the reflection of his own square and essentially pleasant face, his brown eyes, and thick, reddish hair.

People who smiled surreptitiously at him when he repeated their words also made him angry. He had been told by many people that he had the annoying habit of repeating the words and sentences of those to whom he was speaking, but he could never remember doing it. Consequently, when people smiled at him for it, he had no idea why they were smiling – he thought they were amused by him, or that they harboured a secret they weren't sharing, and so he got angry, and he saw himself doing some quick, efficient, and bloody act of violence to them. But this was an impulse he had never acted upon because he was almost religiously concerned with being a civilized man, and with reacting in a civilized way to all that went on around him.

'It's called echolalia,' Sylvia told him. 'Jack, you have echolalia.'

'Echolalia,' he said.

She smiled. 'See? There, that's what I mean. You repeated what I said.'

'No, I didn't.'

'But you did, Jack.'

'No, I didn't,' he said, which was another facet of the problem: sometimes he repeated his *own* words.

Now, at the age of thirty-seven, his echolalia seemed to be fading, he thought. Or maybe people

had gotten used to it, so there were fewer surrep-
titious smiles.

He also felt an impulse to violence when he ate.
But this was a different sort of impulse than the
impulse he felt when he looked in a mirror, or caught
people smiling surreptitiously.

His sister Lila noticed one Thanksgiving – and not
for the first time – that he seemed tense as he ate his
turkey and cranberries and mashed potatoes, and she
told him later that she thought he looked like he was
protecting his food.

'Protecting my food?' he said.

'Sure,' she said. 'So no one will steal it.'

'Steal it,' he said, and then added, 'Who's going to
steal my food?'

She said, 'How often do you eat out?'

'Eat out?'

'With friends.'

'Friends.' He thought a moment. 'What friends?'

'I know you have friends, Jack. Everyone has
friends.'

'They do?'

'Of course. What about the people you work
with?'

'Work with?' He thought a moment. 'They're just
people at work, Lila.'

'But don't you ... go out to lunch with your
buddies? Don't all men do that? Don't you go to a bar
and have lunch?'

'No.'

'That's very sad,' she said.

'Sad,' said Erthmun. 'I don't know. Is it?'

She assured him that it was sad.

He said, no, it wasn't, and that he didn't feel sad.

Two

Decades earlier, in another place
The man is tall, athletically built, ruddy complexioned; he's accustomed to spending numberless hours tending his fields. Until recently, his daughter has spent her days being home-schooled by her mother, the man's wife. But the man is alone, now, except for his daughter, and his wife lies in her grave, a victim of disease.

It's a hot and sunny day as the man works. His daughter stands by, wishing she could be helpful, and wondering why she can't simply stay at the house while he works, or, indeed, go to the school, which is accessible by bus. His explanations have been unsatisfactory. 'I'm sorry, Greta, but the other children aren't like you,' and, 'I don't want you alone in the house.'

A noisy crow flies over. Man and child look idly at

it, and when it is gone, the man clutches his chest. He has been using a spade to dislodge a large rock; the spade falls to the ground.

The man's pain fades slowly; he lets go of his chest and turns to his daughter. 'That's not a word I want you to repeat, Greta,' he says. 'That's not a word to repeat.'

The child looks on in confusion. 'Yes, Father,' she says.

The pain returns and the tall man curses again, and again, and when the pain subsides, he says once more, 'Not a word to repeat. Not a word – ' But the pain renews itself and chokes off the sentence.

The man slumps, groaning, to his knees.

'Father?' the child cries out. 'Father?'

The man's pain subsides, but only a little, and it occurs to him all at once that he's dying. His acceptance of his own death is quick, almost casual, because he knows that there is a more important consideration – his daughter will be left alone at the secluded farmhouse.

The man's pain returns, and a quivering smile that's designed to show affection and concern, confusion and resignation all at the same time shivers along the tall man's lips.

Then he curses once and falls face forward onto the wet earth.

In the last few weeks, the rain has been nearly continuous, and the earth gives testimony to it. All about, the things that come out of the earth are showing themselves. The thickets bordering the field are a vibrant green, and the small pine forest to the west – all winter and spring no more than a monotone darkness – seems in motion, as if in anticipation of summer and the changes it will bring.

'Father?' the child cries. 'Father?'

The tall man lies still. A burying beetle – small and efficient – probes at his chin.

And around the tall man, the earth lives, the earth produces, and swells a little in expectation of what this recent death will give it (only one of many thousands of deaths that moment).

'Get up, Father,' the child says.

The child waits. What she has known from her father until this moment has been life. She has seen him strain for hours at a stuck plough. She has seen him smile wearily at the end of the day. She has heard curses from him, and, each time, 'Not a word to repeat, Greta. Not a word to repeat.' And, until recently, she has heard him in the act of love – the act of life.

'Father? Get up, Father.' There was some small magic in the words, before. There is no magic, now.

Night comes.

The child continues to wait.

There's more bewilderment than grief in the child, now. Around her, things that the earth has produced are becoming bold with curiosity. One creature is within arm's reach, but – and not because of the moonless dark – the child does not sense its presence.

The creature waits. Because of all that the earth has produced in recent weeks, its belly is full, and so it is merely curious. After many minutes, it moves off.

The child continues to wait.

Other things that the earth has produced – some as large as the child, some larger, and some so small she could not see them, even in daylight – move closer and form a rough circle around the child and the tall man. Still, the child is ignorant of their presence.

The child waits. Eventually, the moonless dark lightens; a false dawn, but the end of darkness.

'Father?' she says. 'Father?' The word is so mechanical, now, that she does not realize she's said it.

She turns, hesitates, looks back at the grey and elongated mass that is her father.

And she goes back to the empty farmhouse.

It's very quiet in the house, now. It is a maze of black and grey and harsh right angles. Habit soon overcomes the maze, and the child makes her way to the house's second floor, to her bedroom, and settles onto the old bed. Tears come to her, though she can't yet consciously admit that there is reason for tears. They trickle down the sides of her face.

The house is creative. Occasionally, there are new and often fleeting noises whose source is hard to pinpoint. Only half-consciously, the child listens to just such noises now. And waits, expectation growing in her.

After a long moment, she calls, 'Father? Is that you?' She props herself up in the bed and continues to listen. She strains to see, but sees little.

'Father?' she repeats, though with uncertainty, because the noises her father's footfalls make on the stairs are of a different sort – they are more pronounced, and more purposeful.

The noises stop.

The child sleeps.

The morning

Realization, like punishment, comes swiftly to the child, and, as to punishment, she winces and stifles a moan. Here, in the bright sunlight, denial is impossible. She sees that her father's body is becoming what swamps are made of, and soil is made of – becoming food for the horsetail, and clover, the burying beetles, and a million others. Because the earth, the breathing earth, must be constantly nourished.

Her father's words are closer now, and understandable. 'Decay is not the grim thing it appears to be. It is renewal.'

'Father?' the child pleads, realizing the futility of the word. 'Father?' she repeats, more in memory of those times when her father responded to the word than for any other reason.

Father? – distantly, from the thickets to the south. *Father?* – barely audible.

The child looks up questioningly from her father's body. 'Father?' she calls.

Father?

An echo, the child thinks. Months before, she remembers, in the heart of the forest – 'Hello,' extended, 'Hello,' repeated, 'Hello,' shouted back at both of them, father and daughter, by the voices of the forest.

'Hello,' the child calls.

Father? replies the voice of the thickets.

'Hello,' the child calls. And distantly, from the east, from the forest, *Hello, Hello, Hello*, decreasing in volume, and finally, nothing.

Hello – from the thickets.

'Hello,' the child calls.

Hello.

'Hello, Father!' the child calls.

And the forest replies, *Hello, Father! Hello, Father!*

And the voice of the thickets replies, *Hello, Father! Father? Hello!*

Three

Erthmun lived alone in a three-room, fourth-floor apartment in Manhattan's West Village. His building was sturdy, old and dreary, and the other people who shared the building with him were of various ages and occupations: one was an assistant editor at *Elle* magazine, another was a postal worker, another a retired professor of biochemistry; several were self-proclaimed artists and writers looking for their big break in the city that had been known to give big breaks to others like them. All of these people nodded at one another in the hallways and on the elevators, but none had struck up friendships with anyone else in the building.

Erthmun kept no pets. He had long ago found that he possessed a strange ambivalence towards animals, and that they apparently possessed the same sort of ambivalence towards him. He looked with a kind of awe at the stray cats that roamed his neighbourhood, and he thought of them as survivors. He respected them for this, and felt an uneasy kinship with them, but they eyed him warily, as if unsure if he were friend or foe.

Erthmun had been named after a maternal uncle who became a favourite of him and his siblings. Uncle Jack had been a bear of a man who did a lot of hearty laughing and had brought presents whenever he'd visited. He had been partial to Erthmun, but he hid it well.

As an adult, Erthmun was haunted by the memory of Uncle Jack's death. The man's last words, heard only by Erthmun himself, were 'Oh, shit!' Uncle Jack said this as if at a fleeting annoyance – a missed turn while driving, a name forgotten, a passing shower on a sunny day. Erthmun thought that it was a strange attitude in the face of death – annoyance – and found himself ashamed of Uncle Jack for it. He would have preferred that the man died kicking and screaming in anger because his life was coming to an end. What else was there, after all, but life?

Uncle Jack was also a man who told stories that made his young nieces huddle together in delicious fright, and caused Erthmun himself to stand at his bedroom window for hours on end in search of the marvellous and misty and dangerous creatures that, according to Uncle Jack, inhabited the hills and fields around the house on Four Mile Creek.

'It's like this,' Uncle Jack said. 'You can't see them

if you're actually *looking* at them. You won't see them that way. That would be too *easy* wouldn't it?' He laughed. 'You can only see them if you're *not* looking at them.'

Eight-year-old Lila said, 'But, Uncle Jack, how can you see them if you don't look at them?'

He laughed again and explained. 'Well, try this one night. Go out and look up at the sky and then find a patch of sky where there doesn't appear to be any stars. Look hard into this patch of black sky, and if you look long enough, after a while, very dim stars will appear, but not exactly where you're looking. These very dim stars will appear only just outside where you're *not* looking.'

Lila smiled. 'I did that once, Uncle Jack.'

'Of course you did,' he said. 'And that's how you see these creatures I'm talking about, too. Because they're so fast, because they run so fast, faster than anything you've ever seen, faster than the wind itself, and because they can look like the things around them – they can look like the grass, or the trees, or the sky and the clouds – you can't see them unless you look just ahead of them or just behind them.'

'Behind them,' Erthmun said; it wasn't a question.

'Behind them,' Uncle Jack repeated. 'Or above them, even.'

Lila said, wide-eyed, 'What do they look like, Uncle Jack?'

'They look like you' – he touched her nose gently – 'and you' – he touched Erthmun's nose – 'and you'

– Sylvia's nose. He laughed again. 'And some of them even look like me!'

Lila, still wide-eyed, asked, 'Where do they come from, Uncle Jack?'

'Well, Lila,' Uncle Jack said, 'where does *anything* come from?'

'Where does anything come from?' Erthmun said.

'I don't know,' Lila said, clearly perplexed.

'From heaven,' Sylvia offered.

'From heaven,' Erthmun said.

'From *every*where,' Uncle Jack declared, and gave them all his biggest and wisest smile.

'From *every*where,' Erthmun said.

'*Every*where!' Lila said, as if in awe.

Erthmun was a homicide detective in Manhattan's Twentieth Precinct. He was almost preternaturally good at his work, but his methods had aroused suspicion among the powers-that-be because, as far as everyone else was concerned, Erthmun's ideas of 'probable cause' for search and arrest warrants amounted to no more than hunches.

PARTIAL TRANSCRIPT OF CRIMINAL TRIAL HELD AT RICHMOND COUNTY SUPERIOR COURT, STATEN ISLAND, 1993:

C.E. (Counsel for the Defense): Could you describe what you saw there, Detective Erthmun, at the end of the driveway, that morning, when you arrived at 18 Morningside Lane?

Jack Erthmun: 18 Morningside Lane? Yes, sir. I saw the body of a very obese Caucasian male dressed in a white shirt, black pants and black shoes. He was lying on his stomach, and there appeared to be a bullet wound at the base of his neck—

C.E.: Did you do a direct examination of this wound, Detective, to determine if it was an exit wound or an entrance wound?

J.E.: Not as such. No, sir.

C.E.: Why not?

J.E.: Why not? I didn't think it was necessary.

C.E.: You didn't think it was necessary?

J.E.: Yes, sir.

C.E.: You didn't think it was necessary to determine whether or not this wound, which was apparently the victim's cause of death, occurred as the result of a bullet fired from in front of the victim, or from behind the victim?

P.K. (Assistant District Attorney): Objection. Asked and answered.

J.W. (Judge): Sustained. Ask a new question, Counselor.

C.E.: Could you tell the court, Detective, why you didn't think it was important to discover whether or not the wound was an exit wound or an entrance wound?

J.E.: Yes, sir. I knew that the victim had been killed by a bullet that entered his body from the front.

C.E.: I'm sorry, Detective. You're going to have to

explain that. You *knew* [emphasis] that the bullet
had entered from the front *before* [emphasis] you
actually examined the body? Is that what you're
telling the court?

J.E.: Yes.

C.E.: How did you know this, Detective?

J.E.: Know this? I knew because of the victim's
[witness hesitates] demeanor.

C.E.: His demeanor? Could you explain that,
Detective?

J.E.: Not in so many words. No.

C.E.:   Do the best you can, Detective.

J.E.: I am. I am.

C.E.: [to the Judge]: Your Honor, could you please
instruct the witness to answer my question.

J.W.: [to witness]: Detective, could you please
answer Counselor's questions as fully as possible,
within the bounds of your expertise.

J.E.: I am, Your Honor.

J.W.: Could you explain, Detective, the word
'demeanor' as you have used it here in reference to
the victim?

J.E.: [hesitates] I would have to say that it was in
the nature of . . . instinct, Your Honor.

J.W.: Please direct your answers to Counsel,
Detective.

J.E.: Yes, I'm sorry. [To counsel] It was instinct.
Instinct.

C.E.: That's not acceptable, Detective. You're
going to have to be a whole lot more forthcoming

with this court. [Hesitates.] I'm unclear as to what you mean by the demeanor of the victim. Could you explain to the court why you didn't do a direct examination of the victim's neck wound to discover if it was an entrance or an exit wound?

P.K.: Objection. Asked and answered.

J.W.: Sustained. Let's move on, Counselor.

C.E.: Your Honor, I am trying to establish why the witness didn't try to determine the nature of this wound. I think it hinges on competence, Your Honor.

J.W.: I understand that. But I have sustained Counsel's objection. Let's move on.

C.E.: Detective, when you say that you took notice of the victim's demeanor, what exactly do you mean?

J.E.: Mean? I'm not sure.

C.E.: Give it your best shot, Detective.

J.E.: I'm not sure. I mean [witness hesitates] I mean that the victim, within the crime scene, was [witness hesitates] expressive. Expressive.

C.E.: In what way was the victim expressive, Detective?

J.E.: I think in a holistic way. The victim at the crime scene was expressive in a holistic way.

C.E.: Detective, are you trying to be confrontational?

P.K.: Objection.

J.W.: No, I think I agree with Counsel. [To witness] Detective, your answers to Counsel's questions are unresponsive. I must admonish you that you are under oath and that you must answer Counsel's questions as directly and as truthfully as possible.

J.E.: As truthfully as possible. Yes, Your Honor.

C.E.: Thank you, Your Honor. [To witness] Isn't it true, Detective, that your methods of investigation have been described as unusual?

P.K.: Objection. Described by whom?

J.W.: Sustained.

C.E.: Detective, would you say that your methods of investigation are unusual?

P.K.: Objection. Calls for speculation.

J.W.: Sustained. Rephrase your question, Counsel.

Erthmun thought that dead bodies were exquisite. They were so articulate, so passionless and yet so passionate. They spoke volumes, not only about the victim, but about the perpetrator, too – all in shades of red and pink and white and brown.

Many decades earlier, in another place
The creature had passed this way weeks before, when there had been rain and wind. The combination had produced a sharp, numbing coldness.

Today, the sun was bright and warm, and a little breeze played with the fine, light brown hairs on the creature's arms and legs.

The creature was alive.

He had been alive, as well, in the rain and wind, when the numbness had crept over him, and he had felt pain, and a round, aching darkness had formed at the front of his consciousness.

He remembered the pain now, and his muscles tensed as if that time were the present. The darkness – his ignorance of what was happening to him – formed once more.

And almost before it started, almost before the creature had time to realize it had started, it ended. And the warm sunlight, and sensual breezes made his nerves and muscles sing.

He was new to the earth. He had much to learn, much to experience, and very little time to do it before the killing winter came. Thousands had sprung up before him, over the span of half a thousand years. Most had withered and died before a season was through. Those lives and those deaths dwelt within him. If he had looked, he would have seen what those who had gone before had seen, and he would have felt what they felt, and he would have found knowledge in what they saw. He would have found power, too.

But he didn't bother to look.

Because, for now, he was being caressed. The earth – which was both his mother and his father – was caressing him. Just as it had nursed him, and had given him life, and pain, and dizzying pleasure.

Four

Early winter
The snow was deep and grey in Manhattan, and the air was cold, still and dense. It smelled of exhaust fumes, deli sandwiches, urine. Erthmun's joints hurt on days as cold as this. He had thought often of moving south and, as often as he had thought of it, he had wondered why he simply didn't do it.

He was in a dreary little park at East 77th Street and Avenue C, and he was looking at a body lying in the snow. The body was that of a white male, about thirty-five years old, clean-shaven, black-haired. It was dressed for winter, in a bright blue parka and heavy pants, orange mittens, and a red cap with a tassel. It lay face up, arms wide, left leg bent. The body wore black buckle boots, and a rictus grin that had snow in it. The eyes were open, and they were muddy grey and green. There were no obvious signs of violence, and no clear indication as to the cause of the man's death. He looked as though he had simply fallen asleep in the snow.

The little park was bordered by a tall, wrought-iron fence. There were various posters on this fence, and they advertised strip shows, night clubs, off-Broadway plays. They were attached to the fence by strips of wire or tape. The borough of Manhattan was supposed to see to the maintenance of the park, which included keeping posters off the fence, but this was unimportant work in a city that had much larger problems, so it was work that did not get done.

Erthmun, who was kneeling over the body of the man in the snow, nodded at one of the posters, and said to a uniformed cop standing nearby, 'Could you get that for me, please?'

The cop looked in the direction Erthmun had nodded, but wasn't sure what Erthmun was talking about. 'Get what?' he said.

'Get what?' Erthmun said. 'That yellow poster. Bring it to me.'

The cop said, 'Sure,' and did as he was asked.

Erthmun studied the poster a moment. It advertised a revue playing in SoHo called *The Brown Bag Blues*. The letters were in black script. A graphic of a naked woman caressing the letter S in the word *Blues* was in purple. Erthmun gave the poster back to the uniformed cop and said, 'Get me that one,' and pointed at a smaller poster.

Erthmun's partner was a tall, long-haired woman

who dressed well, in tweeds and trendy hats. Her name was Patricia David and she had been standing at the other end of the body in the snow during Erthmun's exchange with the uniformed cop. She smiled – although Erthmun couldn't see it because he was looking at the uniformed cop – and said, 'What are you up to, Jack?'

Erthmun said, without looking at her, 'I don't know.' It was the truth.

The uniformed cop came back and handed Erthmun a white poster. Erthmun looked at it. Patricia David came around the body to look at it, too. She read the poster aloud, 'Mortality Makes Mulch of us All.' She grinned. 'Pithy.'

Erthmun glanced silently at her, then looked at the poster again. The brown words on a white background were neatly handwritten and they were the only words on the poster. They were arranged with the word 'Mortality' as the first line, 'Makes Mulch' on the second, and 'of us All' on the third. There was not a lot of blank space on the poster; the margins were narrow, left and right, top and bottom, and a small, hand-drawn graphic of a devil's head lay at the bottom centre. Erthmun stared at this devil's head. He touched it, felt nothing. The words and graphic had been done with a marking pen. He held the poster to his nose, sniffed, smelled the unmistakable and stinging aroma of marker ink.

Patricia David said, 'Do you think that's important, Jack?'

He looked at her – he had his mouth open a little, like a dog savouring an odour. He closed it and said, 'You mean smelling this poster?'

She shook her head and gave him a quick, long-suffering kind of smile: when Erthmun was caught up in the beginning of an investigation, he often became unresponsive, sometimes even surly. She accepted this as part of his investigative technique, which she respected.

'No, that poster,' she said. 'Do you think it's important?'

Erthmun shrugged. 'It's important? I don't know. I don't think so.'

The uniformed cop said, 'They're all over the city.'

'Yes, I know,' Erthmun said, and handed the poster to Patricia David. 'Put this in the car, would you?'

She scowled, took the poster from him, said, 'When we're done here, *then* I'll put it in the car.'

Erthmun nodded distractedly – he hadn't heard the annoyance in her voice – and turned back to the body. He thought that the snow had melted from the man's rictus grin. This was odd. Surely the body hadn't gotten warmer. He glanced questioningly at Patricia David, then at the body again. He saw that he had been mistaken. The snow hadn't melted from the man's rictus grin.

He bent over and put his ear to the man's mouth, as if the man were going to whisper to him.

'Christ,' said the uniformed cop, 'what in the hell is he doing?'

Patricia David said nothing.

Erthmun straightened and held out his hand for the white poster. Patricia gave it to him; he stared hard at it for a long moment, then gave it back. 'Could you put that in the car?' he said again.

She sighed. 'When we *go* back to the car, Jack, *then* I'll—'

'Yes,' he cut in. 'I'm sorry.' He looked down at the body and said nothing for a full minute. Patricia David and the uniformed cop glanced questioningly at one another. At last Erthmun said, 'I'm very hungry.'

'You're *hungry*?' Patricia said incredulously.

Erthmun pointed at the dead man's stomach. 'Hungry? He's very hungry.'

The uniformed cop whispered, 'Shit.'

'Shit,' Erthmun whispered.

Patricia said, 'What do you mean he's hungry, Jack?'

He shook his head. 'I don't know.' It was the truth. He bent over the man's body again, and put his hand on its belly. He hesitated, then pushed hard. The snow around the man's mouth fluttered; a dime-sized clot of snow fell from the man's lips.

'Jesus Christ,' said the uniformed cop.

'Jack, is there a reason for all this?' Patricia asked.

Erthmun did not answer. He pushed on the man's belly again, harder, with similar results. A small groan escaped from the man's throat – his vocal cords responding to the passage of air.

Erthmun straightened, shook his head, as if in

confusion, glanced at Patricia David, then looked at the dead man's face again. 'Did anyone call the Medical Examiner?'

Patricia David said, 'Jack, you're the detective in charge, that's up to you.'

Erthmun looked blankly at her a moment, then said, 'Oh, sure.' He glanced at the uniformed cop. 'Call him, would you?'

The uniformed cop said, 'Right away,' and went to his patrol car.

Erthmun bent over the body again, sniffed at the dead man's mouth, and, again, his own mouth opened a little.

Patricia David said, 'Something, Jack?'

He whispered, his lips close to the man's nose, 'It was a stupid thing you did, my friend.'

Five

Many decades earlier, in another place

A man stood and moved a few feet along the trunk of the fallen tree. The trillium was in greater abundance here than in any other part of the forest. Ivy snaked through the branches closest to the earth, and, on the east side of the trunk, just below where the branches started, a large growth of yellow-brown shelf fungus had established itself. In a large, roughly circular area below the fungus, jutting out of the covering of leaves and pine needles, was a growth of puffballs. The man smiled nostalgically and bent over for a close look. He saw that these puffballs were a lighter colour than he remembered from childhood, that they closely resembled the colour of his own skin. Surely this was an illusion. The approaching storm had doubtless caused the light to change. His hands, his normally blue coveralls, even the grey trunk of the fallen tree bore a slightly orange cast.

In an effort to shield it from the sickly, all-pervasive light of the coming storm, the man cupped his hands over one of the puffballs. Its colour altered slightly. He straightened, and, unthinkingly, kicked at it. He realized, as his kick landed, that he'd done that same thing years before, because the puffballs, bulging with spores, exploded delightfully. This one didn't. As he watched, it slowly and grotesquely lost its shape. First the side that he'd kicked, then the rounded top, then the far sides, as if the weight of some invisible animal were upon it. Finally, it lay at his feet like a crumpled piece of thin, discoloured leather, and the wind blew bits of long-dead leaves over it.

Six

Erthmun did not believe that the dead actually spoke to him. He did not believe that the corpse in the bright blue parka and orange mittens had told him in so many words about the balloons filled with cocaine that he had swallowed. Erthmun did not, in fact, believe in an afterlife, in heaven, hell, or in the talking dead. He believed that the corpse in the bright blue parka was eloquent in the way that the earth itself was eloquent, because that, after all, was what the corpse was returning to – the earth. It – the earth – had created the man. The man had died – because one of the cocaine-filled balloons in his stomach had broken open – and now the corpse that had once been a man was becoming one with the earth again. This was a fact as obvious to Erthmun as the fact of gravity, but he had never tried to share it with anyone. He wasn't sure why not. He thought it may

have been because most of the people he knew – the
people he worked with; his social life was non-
existent – seemed to have their own strongly held
beliefs, which were not much in tune with his own.
And he could see no need to convince others that his
beliefs were more valid than theirs, even though he
knew, of course, that they were.

In winter, Erthmun kept his apartment very hot. He
had received complaints about this from the tenant
above him, a young and overweight man named
Henry.

'Why do you keep your apartment so fucking hot?'
Henry asked once.

'I need to,' Erthmun answered. He was not a man
who engaged in long explanations of his eccentric
behaviour because, simply enough, he did not view it
as eccentric.

'Well, maybe you want to pay my fucking air-
conditioning bill, then!' Henry said.

'Why would I want to do that?' Erthmun said.

Henry sputtered something incoherent and went
away. He did not speak to Erthmun again because he
thought Erthmun was crazy. 'He's got a maniacal
glint in his eye,' he told his friends.

Erthmun slept naked under several blankets and
quilts, even when his apartment was hot. He slept
naked because he did not believe there was any other
right way to sleep. In sleep, he maintained, we are

drawn closer to the earth, and because we sprang naked from the earth, that was the way the earth wanted us to sleep. He slept deeply, and long, and was difficult to awaken. And he claimed also that he never dreamed. People told him that this was incorrect, that he indeed did dream but simply did not remember his dreams. His sister Lila explained, 'We dream once every fourteen minutes, Jack. This is empirical fact. If we did not dream, then we would drive ourselves into insanity. I believe that all mammals dream. It's nature's safety valve.'

'No,' Erthmun maintained. 'I don't dream. I never have.' But this was not true. He did remember his dreams, though his dreams were not the kind that most people had. He dreamed variously that he was a clump of earth, a root, a worm, a rock. And because such things as clumps of earth, rocks, roots and worms have no real intelligence or memory, when he woke he had no recollection of these dreams.

He tired completely, to the point of exhaustion. This happened once a day, and it happened quickly. He ate voraciously – rare meat (beef, lamb, poultry), green vegetables, carrots, potatoes, berries, fruit – read his evening paper, and then stripped, turned up the heat, and went to bed. Sleep always overtook him within seconds.

He was a very sexual man. He always woke with an erection. He got an erection when he saw an attractive woman. He got an erection when men he worked with talked about a previous evening's conquest. He got an erection when Patricia David walked away from him to go back to her desk, or walked in front of him on the way to the car. It was her rear end that he liked most.

He wasn't a virgin, but he had never had a sexual encounter that he felt was totally satisfying because he was prone to premature ejaculation. Often, he ejaculated before intercourse began. Ejaculation was a great joy for him, premature or not, but he understood the needs of his partner, too. So, after apologies were made, he often helped his partner to achieve orgasm. This made him feel that his premature ejaculation was not as much of a problem as others apparently thought it was. Besides, wasn't it true that humans were the only species who carried on with intercourse for more than a couple of seconds? Look at dogs, cats, squirrels, rhinos, lions. Didn't they get the whole thing finished as quickly as possible? Many of these creatures engaged in extended foreplay, it was true, but foreplay wasn't intercourse, and foreplay wasn't ejaculation.

This night, the night that the man in the bright blue parka was being autopsied, Erthmun's phone rang while he slept. He did not sleep through a ringing telephone, but he did not wake at once, either. Those who knew him understood that, if they called him while he was sleeping, they would have to let his phone ring a couple of dozen times, and that, even after he answered it, he might not be completely available for rational conversation for several minutes.

'Erthmun,' he said when at last he answered the telephone.

'Jack, this is Patricia. Are you awake?'

'Awake? No.'

'When will you *be* awake?'

'How can I answer that? How can I answer that?'

'Jack, wake up.'

'I'm awake.'

'No, you're not.'

'I'm talking to you. I'm awake.'

She sighed. This kind of somnolent logic was hard to counter. She said, 'What are you doing now?'

'Now? Nothing.'

'You're *talking* to me Jack. I called you and you're talking to me. Now wake up. This is important.'

'I am awake.'

Another sigh. 'Jack, we've got work to do.'

'I am working. I'm *working*!'

'You're *sleeping*, for Christ's sake!'

'For Christ's sake! That can't be. How can that be?' More somnolent logic.

'Jack, get up, get a drink of water, look out the window—'

'Get up, get a drink of water, look out the window. Who can do all that? Who can do all that?'

And so it went. It took another fifteen minutes before Erthmun was awake and responding lucidly.

**TEXT OF A REPORT WRITTEN BY OFFICER GORDON
LOW SUBMITTED TO MANHATTAN SUPERIOR COURT
ON THE INVESTIGATION OF A MURDER AT 9TH STREET
WEST AND AVENUE B IN 1992**

Detective Erthmun arrived on the crime scene at
approximately 10:30 p.m. on the night of August 12.
He did not appear to be drunk or under the influence
of drugs. He said hello to this officer and to the other
officers then on the scene and did not look at the
body immediately but looked through the apartment
very briefly. After he had done this, he went out on
the balcony and stood on it for approximately 15
minutes. This officer doesn't know what Detective
Erthmun was doing on the balcony because the light
was low there. Then Detective Erthmun came into
the apartment but still did not look directly at the
body but asked this officer if there was anyone else
in the apartment. I told the Detective that there was
no one else in the apartment and then he shook my
hand. He appeared to be trying to avoid looking at
the body and this officer asked the Detective if
something was wrong. Detective Erthmun said that
everything was okay. Then he went and talked to the
other uniformed officers who were on the scene.
There were three other uniformed officers. They
were officers Grady, Bord, and Winde. There was
also another detective, but she was there in an
unofficial capacity as a homicide trainee, and her
name was Patricia David. She was standing in the
dining area of the apartment.

This officer overheard Detective Erthmun ask one of the officers if the coroner had been called and the other officer told Detective Erthmun that he was not empowered to do that but Detective Erthmun was empowered to do that. Detective Erthmun nodded and this officer overheard him say that he knew that he was empowered to call the coroner and then he apologized for his confusion.

Detective Erthmun then turned only his head so he could look at the victim's body. The victim's body was behind the Detective at this point in time. The Detective looked at the victim for approximately five minutes. The Detective did not appear to move his body during this time. The Detective's facial expression appeared to change during this time. It became an expression of anger. That is, his eyes narrowed and his lips grew tight. His hands became fists during this time, as well. This officer came forward and asked the Detective if there was a problem but the Detective did not answer except to the extent that the Detective repeated verbatim what this officer had said to him.

Then the Detective bent over the murder victim, who was on her back, so the Detective's face was very close to the victim's face. The victim's eyes were open.

Then the Detective appeared to this officer to look into the victim's eyes. Then the Detective's mouth moved as if he was talking, but this officer did not hear any words.

This mouth movement continued for several minutes and then the Detective bent over further so that his ear was close to the victim's mouth, which was open. Then the Detective stood up and he motioned to Detective David to come over, which she did.

At this point in time, Detective Erthmun said to Detective Trainee David that the victim had told him that it was 'unfortunate about failed relationships' and that the investigation of the crime should center on the victim's most recent boyfriend. Detective David seemed incredulous about this, although she said nothing directly to Detective Erthmun within this officer's hearing.

Seven

A thousand deaths happened that day. Most of the deaths went unnoticed, except by those who killed, and those who died. The city survived because of the dead; the dead made room for the living, and the children and grandchildren of the living.

Near the edge of the city, at the perimeter of a landfill, in a place where they would not be seen, two brothers laboriously dug a deep hole and then dumped the body of a middle-aged hooker into it. The hooker had died at their hands; the reasons didn't matter.

In Harlem, a man barely in his twenties leaped from the top floor of his tenement house and died instantly when he hit the pavement, fifteen storeys below.

On East Houston Street, in The Bowery, a sanitation engineer standing too far out in the street, waiting for his co-worker to return with a load of garbage, was clipped by a passing taxi and sent sprawling head first into a street sign. He broke his neck.

In the Holland Tunnel, a woman on her way out of Manhattan to visit her daughter in New Jersey, began swiping furiously at a bee on the inside of her windshield and hit another car head-on. A gasoline tanker, just behind her, jack-knifed into the wreckage and exploded within seconds. The resulting inferno killed a dozen people, and sent another dozen to various hospitals in Manhattan.

In Greenwich Village, a four-year-old boy playing with his father's .38 pointed the weapon at his mother, said, 'Bang!' and pulled the trigger. The bullet lodged in his mother's lung; she died four hours later of massive haemorrhaging.

These were the kinds of deaths that happened regularly in the city. And those who paid attention to them would merely shake their heads and cluck that accidents happened all the time, there was really nothing anybody could do about it, or they'd whisper that the Mafia had its hands into everything, or proclaim that they'd never have a gun in *their* house.

These were the kinds of deaths that people could deal with. In a sense, they were a form of entertainment.

The stairwell where the woman's body lay smelled of shit, urine, blood, hairspray and chocolate. The combination of odours made Patricia David retch. She gave the body a cursory glance, made her apologies and said she had to leave the building for a moment. Erthmun said, 'Sure, I understand', though in his heart he didn't, and bent over the body. He did not find the odours here as off-putting as Patricia did. He liked chocolate – he was all but addicted to it. And here, in the stairwell, the overpowering smell of the stuff came from the victim's open mouth, which had had a good half-pound of dark chocolate jammed into it. Some had melted around the woman's lips, but most of it was still intact.

Erthmun stood close to the body and stared. There were several uniformed cops nearby; he glanced at one of them and said, 'What do you think this is? Hershey's?'

The cop shrugged. 'Who knows?'

Erthmun turned back to the victim. 'It's cheap chocolate,' he said. 'It's too sweet – you can smell that it's too sweet. It isn't Perugina or Godiva.'

Patricia David reappeared. He glanced at her. 'This is cheap chocolate,' he said.

She nodded grimly.

Erthmun straightened a little, though he was still bent over the body. It was naked and it had been hacked up so completely that blood covered it like a body stocking. Even the long hair was covered with it. Its natural colour may have been blonde, Erthmun thought, but he couldn't be sure. The pretty, oval face, however, looked as if it had been meticulously cleaned and the pale skin here, contrasted with the nearly total covering of blood on the body and hair, was jarring.

Erthmun said, to no one in particular, 'She looks like a mime, a mime.' He bent over the body again and stared into its open eyes, which were bright jade green. 'Beautiful,' he said. 'I don't think I've ever seen eyes quite this colour before.'

'Those are contacts,' Patricia told him.

He glanced quickly at her, then at the victim's eyes again. 'Are they?' he said, but it was a rhetorical question, and Patricia thought for a moment that Erthmun was toying with her, although that would have been unlike him. She knew him as a man to whom humour was not a necessity of everyday living.

He asked, 'What do you think did this?' He was still looking at the body.

'You mean the murder weapon?' Patricia said, and gave the body a quick once-over. 'It wasn't an axe, or a hatchet. That's obvious. The wounds are too narrow.'

'Too narrow,' Erthmun said, and asked, without looking at Patricia, 'Some kind of sword, then?'

She shrugged, began to answer, and Erthmun cut in, 'Do you want to leave the building, again?' He glanced around at her. She thought he looked genuinely concerned. She shook her head quickly.

He said, 'I think you do.'

'No. You're wrong.' She gestured at the body. 'Let's concentrate on what we're doing here, okay?'

'You're angry,' Erthmun said. 'Why are you angry?'

'Jack, please—'

'It wasn't a sword,' he interrupted. 'The wounds are all of a uniform length. See here.' He pointed at a bright red gash on the woman's left arm. 'That's what? Six inches.' He pointed at a similar gash on her right arm. 'Six inches here, too.' He pointed at her belly. 'And here.' He pointed first at her right thigh, then her left, both of which bore similar gashes of similar lengths. 'And they're all the same depth, too.' He was smiling, now, and this made Patricia uncomfortable because she wasn't sure why he was smiling, and because he so seldom smiled.

Erthmun declared, 'This is a very ritualistic thing. Someone has made this woman up with her own blood, her own blood!' He straightened suddenly. His smile became a flat grin. 'Look at her! Look at her! She's been made up with her own blood! It's a religious thing! Some religious person has done this!' He stared at Patricia. His eyes were wide, his grin flat. He looked like a madman. 'A priest or a rabbi has done this!' he declared. 'Or a shaman! A shaman!'

'Jack, if this is supposed to be funny . . .' Patricia said. She had never seen him like this.

'Supposed to be funny . . .' he said, and stooped over again so that his face was close to the dead woman's. He stared into her bright jade green eyes and whispered hoarsely, 'What's going on here?' He grabbed her hard by the shoulders.

'Jack?' Patricia shouted. 'For Christ's sake, don't do that!'

'Tell me something, dammit!' Erthmun whispered at the dead woman. He shook her by the shoulders. Her head flopped backward, forward, backward. Bits of chocolate flew from her mouth.

'Jack, are you nuts?' Patricia shouted.

Erthmun stood with the dead woman. He held her erect by the shoulders. Her arms were tight against her sides, because of his strong grip on her, and her knees were bent a little because her feet were touching the floor. Her head flopped left, right, backward.

'Put her *down*, Jack!' Patricia shouted.

'. . . *down*, Jack!' Erthmun echoed. He shook the dead woman. 'Talk to me!' he yelled. '*Talk* to me!' He was splattered with her coagulated blood now because her body had bumped against his chest. 'Talk to me, talk to me, Goddammit, talk to me!'

Patricia grabbed his arm. 'Jack, put her down! What in the hell are you doing?'

'Talk to me!' Erthmun yelled into the dead woman's face. 'Talk to me!'

Patricia pulled on his arm. It was no use. He was too strong. She looked frantically at one of the uniformed cops, who was looking on open-mouthed, as if awestruck. 'Help me, for God's sake!' she shouted.

The uniformed cop nodded, came forward quickly, grabbed Erthmun's left wrist.

Erthmun continued shouting at the dead woman, 'Talk to me, Goddammit! Why won't you talk to me?'

Eight

Many decades earlier, in another place
Ten million deaths happened that day. Most of the deaths went unnoticed, except by those who killed and those who died. The forest survived because of the dead. The dead were food for the living, and the children and grandchildren of the living.

Near the edge of the forest, a pair of burying beetles had laboriously dug a hole beneath the corpse of a young bluejay. Earlier in the morning, a crow in search of food for its young had forced the bluejay chick from its nest and had then impaled and lost it. Now the burying beetles were busy pushing dirt over the corpse. They did their work quickly, perhaps aware that the longer the corpse remained visible the greater were the chances that a raccoon or an otter or a fox would come along and snap it up.

From one of the lower branches of an old and

insect-hollowed pine, a great horned owl watched the
burying beetles. His almost constant hunger had been
satisfied. Attached to the back of his neck, by the
teeth, was the rapidly putrefying head of a marsh
mink. What remained of its body lay in the forest
somewhere. The owl had gorged itself on it – once he
had been able to separate it from the head – but the
jaws of the mink were strong and its teeth were
sharp, even now. In time, the head would fall away.

His powerful back legs holding him fast to the petal
of a wild tulip, an ambush bug waited patiently until
a fat honeybee settled on the flower and started the
business of pollination. Then, and although the
ambush bug was only one-tenth the size of the bee, it
attacked, quickly manoeuvred the bee around, stung
it between the eyes, and began its meal. The bee died
five minutes later.

The enemies of the snowshoe hare were numerous.
Besides the owl and the mink, the fox, and the
weasel, they included the ever-present red-tailed
hawk. The forest housed six hawks, and one of them
could always be seen circling just above the trees. The
hare didn't see the one above the clearing until it was
nearly upon him, when the time for escape had long-
since passed.

Near a small pond just beyond the forest's western
perimeter, a praying mantis had hidden himself in a
growth of cat-tails. The mantis was a perfect hunter
and would eat almost anything that it could catch. A
humming-bird, its wings invisible in the dim, early-

morning light, hovered near a bee balm flower not far off. The mantis moved stealthily forward, its powerful legs shot out and it quickly reduced the humming-bird to an unrecognizable mass of feathers and flesh.

Near a cluster of sumac, a growling vixen fed on the carcass of a woodchuck. Her attention was diverted for a moment by a pair of bluejays flying away from the forest. An hour before, two crows had attacked the jays' nest, and now the gutted bodies of four bluejay chicks lay on the ground beneath. One of the bodies had already been found by a burying beetle. Another burying beetle had since joined it. Together, they would dig a hole beneath the bluejay chick and cover it so that none of the other thousands of predators would find it.

Time was not measured here. Though it existed.

Life consumed it.

And death consumed it.

But death is only a servant to life, in all its forms. From the amoeba to the dragonfly, to the owl and the hawk, from the euglena to the wild tulip to the white pine, from the lady's slipper to the death cap mushroom.

Where sun and soil and water combine, there is life.

Nine

In his dream, he was a clump of earth. He was moist, and dark, and he had no memory, and no consciousness, no name and no age. He could not see, or hear, taste, touch, love or hate. He could not become angry or confused, feel pain or joy, loneliness or fear, because he was not yet a living thing. He was a clump of earth.

Then he awoke in a strange place, and remembered nothing of his dream.

Patricia said to him, 'Jack, you did a weird thing.'

A man stood next to her. Erthmun didn't recognize him. He was tall, strongly built, with a thin black moustache and his eyes were small; he wore a grey suit. 'Detective,' he said, 'your partner's right.' His voice was steady and his tone probing and judgemental. 'You did a very weird thing.'

Erthmun said, 'I don't remember, I don't remember.' It was the truth.

Patricia said, 'This is Mark Smalley, from Internal Affairs, Jack.'

'I guessed as much,' Erthmun said. He didn't like looking at the man. Something in his small dark eyes prompted Erthmun's urge to violence and he saw himself, in his mind's eye, springing from the bed and attacking him. He forced the image from his head.

Smalley said, 'Do you know where you are, Detective?'

Erthmun looked around. The walls were beige, the windows narrow, with wire mesh, the floor black and white linoleum squares. 'I'm at Bellevue.'

Smalley nodded. 'That's right, Detective. You're in the psych ward at Bellevue. Do you have any idea why you're here?'

'No,' Jack said. 'I told you, I don't remember, I don't remember.'

Patricia said, 'Do you remember the woman in the stairway, Jack?'

'No.'

Smalley's grin. The grin was humourless, flat and cold, and Erthmun, looking at it, wanted to rip the man's lips from his face. Smalley said, 'Of course you do, Detective. A naked woman with chocolate stuffed in her mouth. Who could forget something like that?'

Erthmun shook his head. 'For Christ's sake, why

don't you stop being coy and simply tell me what it is I'm supposed to have done?'

Patricia told him. When she was finished, he said, 'Why in the hell would I do something like that? I've never done anything like that before.'

'Yes,' Patricia said, 'I know.'

'It's a fucking strange thing to do,' Smalley said drily. 'And that's why you're here.'

'That's why you're here,' Erthmun said. 'So what in the hell does any of this have to do with Internal Affairs?'

Smalley grinned again. 'We think you knew her, Jack.'

In another part of the city, a woman awoke from dreams that she, too, could not remember. She was a stunning woman, with hip-length brown hair, sky-blue eyes, and a face as exquisitely and as preternaturally beautiful as anything that lived.

Like Erthmun, she slept naked, under a cocoon of blankets and quilts, but when she woke, she did not come back from sleep haltingly, as Erthmun did, she came back all at once, as if she had been walking and had simply changed direction.

Blood stained her body, this evening, and when she looked at herself in her mirror and saw the blood, she smiled as if at the memory of something pleasurable. Then she got into her shower, washed off the blood, and soon had forgotten it, and the pleasure.

*

'Knew her,' Erthmun said. 'Knew who?'

'The victim,' Smalley answered. 'The woman with chocolate stuffed in her mouth.'

Patricia asked, '*Did* you know her, Jack?'

Erthmun sighed. 'Of course not. What in the hell makes you think I knew her?'

Smalley said, 'Because you called her by name.'

'By name,' he echoed. 'I did?'

Smalley nodded. 'You called her Helen. That was her middle name. We think it's probably what her friends called her.'

Erthmun shook his head in confusion. 'I don't know anyone named Helen.'

'We want to believe you, Detective,' Smalley said. 'And maybe we do, as far as it goes.'

'Meaning?'

Smalley shook his head a little. 'Shit, I don't know. Maybe I'm just trying to give you the benefit of the doubt. Maybe I'm trying to be magnanimous. They tell me I'm nothing if not magnanimous.' He grinned, glanced quickly at Patricia, who was giving him a puzzled look, then looked at Erthmun again. 'How in the hell can we believe you, Detective? You called the dead woman by name, for Christ's sake. You picked her up and shook her like a rag doll, and you called her "Helen", which was her name. And now you tell us that you don't remember doing it, and that you don't know anyone named Helen. Give me a break, man. I don't think you're stupid, and I know for a fact that I'm not.'

Erthmun fixed on him a steady, unblinking gaze. 'I didn't know her. If you claim that I said these things, then I must have said them. I have no reason to believe that either of you is lying. But I didn't know her.'

'Noreen Helen Obermier,' Smalley said.

After a moment's silence, Erthmun said, 'Yes? And?'

'That was her name.'

'I'll take your word for it.'

'Why do I get the idea that you're not co-operating with this investigation, Detective?'

'Because it's in your nature to be suspicious, I imagine.'

'Damn right. I'm proud of it. It makes me good at what I do.' He grinned again.

Erthmun looked away. His fists were clenched; he closed his eyes tightly. 'Listen,' he said, voice tight, 'I'm tired. Why don't you both get out of here.'

'For now,' Smalley said, and left the room.

'Rest, Jack,' Patricia said.

'Rest, Jack,' Erthmun said. He was released later that day.

When she had dressed, and had lingered at her mirror – because she was fascinated by what she saw reflected in it: she was a creature new to the earth, and most things fascinated her – she ate ravenously of fruit and meat and went out into the night.

She was a creature of the darkness. She loved the

darkness. She saw well in it; she saw many things in it that were hidden to the eyes of others.

She walked with the grace, certainty and stealth of a predator, which, to onlookers, was a sensual walk, alluring and fantastic. It was the walk of sex, which is the walk of power. Men turned to look at her, and women did, too, because she was unlike any human they had ever seen.

Ten

When Mark Smalley interviewed Noreen Helen Obermier's friends and relatives, he found no one who could connect her to Erthmun. This made Smalley confused and angry, because he was certain there was a connection. A man simply doesn't call a dead woman by name if he doesn't know her – Erthmun wasn't psychic, for Christ's sake!

And now he – Smalley – thought it would be smart to begin interviewing Erthmun's relatives. His sister, Lila Grant, lived on Staten Island, and though Smalley could telephone her, he decided it would be best to talk to her in person. He decided this because he was convinced that women could not lie to him face to face. It was clear that he intimidated them because he was tall, strong and athletic, and because he was quick with a one-liner, and not easily surprised. He thought that men often saw this winning combination as a challenge, but that women, even women cops, found his rock hard sensuality, his probing intelligence, his wit and his charm impossible to resist. And although they might try to lie to him, they always gave themselves away – a bat of the eye, a twitch of the hand, a blush, an awkward sideways glance. Sometimes they held his gaze too long, or not long enough. Sometimes, if they were dressed right, he could tell that they were lying because their nipples became erect. He found this fascinating and had wondered if it bore some parallel to male erections and lying. Perhaps all lying was somehow tied to sex. Perhaps all wrongdoing was tied to sex.

He did not telephone Lila Grant first. He hoped to find her at home, but if he didn't then it was all right. He'd come back another day and catch her by surprise.

But she was home. She invited him into her house – after he told her who he was, and after she made him produce his badge to prove it – and led him into her spacious, well-appointed living room. He thought she didn't look at all like Erthmun – she was blonde, thin, very tall – and he wondered if they were really brother and sister.

When he was seated in a Queen Anne loveseat that was too small and straight-backed for anyone's comfort, she said, 'Could I offer you a refreshment of some kind, Detective? Some tea, perhaps, a glass of lemonade?'

He shook his head, said, 'No, thanks, I won't be long. I only have a question or two.'

'As you wish,' she said, smiled graciously, and sat across from him in another Queen Anne loveseat. 'Is Jack in trouble?' she said, still smiling.

'No. There are merely some questions we'd like answered.'

'And that's why you're here, of course.' She was still smiling. It pleased him. People who smiled too much were people who lied.

'Yes,' he said, 'that's why I'm here.'

'You say you're with Internal Affairs, Mr Smalley?'

'That's correct.'

'And you're investigating Jack?'

He nodded. 'Yes.'

'Then he *is* in trouble.' She was still smiling.

Smalley shook his head. Her continuous smiling was beginning to annoy him. 'He's not in trouble, Mrs Grant.'

'But he may soon be in trouble, isn't that right?'

He ignored the question. 'Could you tell me about Jack's friends? Particularly his girlfriends.'

'He doesn't have any.'

'He doesn't have any friends?'

'He doesn't have any girlfriends. Not at the moment, anyway. Actually, I don't think he ever did.'

Smalley cracked a quick smile. Her first lie. 'That's a little hard to believe, Mrs Grant. He's a grown man, after all—'

'I meant that he's never had any lasting relationships, Mr Smalley. He's had one-night stands, of
course. He isn't a choir boy.'

'Of course he isn't.'

The phone rang. Lila Grant turned her body in its
direction for a moment, and Smalley looked at her
breasts. She was wearing a blue satin blouse and they
were large, but she was clearly wearing a bra. He was
disappointed. She turned back. He glanced up quickly
from her breasts to her face, and saw her smile go
crooked for a moment because she had obviously
caught him staring at her and had thought he was
merely being lecherous.

'Excuse me, please,' she said, and went to answer
the telephone.

Erthmun could not remember the face of the dead
woman. He could remember only the smell of the
chocolate that filled her mouth. When he tried to
remember her face, he saw instead the face of another
woman – a face so exquisite it was nearly unreal, as if
it were not a human face at all, but one that existed
only in his imagination.

He was sitting on the edge of his bed. The day was
nearly done, and he was ready for sleep. But he knew
that he wouldn't sleep. He knew that he'd leave the
apartment and that he would look for the woman his
fantasies had shown him. Because he knew that,
unlike him, night was her time.

*

Other than the hunter, that which moves at night is the prey of the hunter – the foolish and the unwary, who laugh and make noise to attract the hunter, who douse themselves with scent and powder so that they can be easily discovered, who dress in clothes that reflect the light and shoes that make them sway like worms, who drink themselves giddy and so become defenceless.

These foolish and unwary were what the earth had given her. These prey were for her sake.

She shivered with excitement. She grew moist, flushed and warm, and she groaned deeply. Her voice was husky and sensual.

Around her in the café people stared. Some were concerned because they thought she was in pain. Others knew well enough that she was not in pain, and they grinned.

One man said, 'I didn't know there was a floor show,' and his friend laughed.

But she heard no laughter, and saw no one staring, because the judgement of others was of no importance to her.

Erthmun's night vision was unusual. If an object was moving then he saw it well, but if it was not it melted into the background of artificial light or shadow and he saw little except vague shapes in ill-defined shades of grey. Consequently, as he walked cars moved past – against the backdrop of store-fronts

and apartment buildings, street signs and garbage
cans – as if against the backdrop of a fog. He had
never questioned this way of seeing because he so
seldom went out at night, and because he had always
assumed that everybody saw the way he did. It was,
after all, the best way to experience the world after
dark. What was more important at night than that
which was moving?

He walked quickly because he was cold. It was not
a particularly cold night – in a city where winter
winds often moved with skin-numbing force through
the corridors between buildings – but that didn't
matter to Erthmun. He was cold because night, simply
enough, was a time for sleep. Night was when the
body shut down and sent its precious heat to the
internal organs so the brain could rest.

Night was a time for only predators and their
prey.

He muttered to himself as he walked. He didn't
know that he was muttering. He didn't hear himself
muttering. Often, during daylight, he had seen others
in this city muttering to themselves and he had
thought them pathetic.

He muttered about his childhood, which was a
mystery to him. He had concocted many fantasies
about it, not so much to solve the mystery as to
push it aside, so that he wouldn't have to deal with
it.

He did not talk loudly, as some in this city did. His

muttering was little more than a whisper, and because there was a good deal of traffic on the Avenue, no one walking nearby could hear him.

'The pine needles make a soft bed,' he muttered. 'I pee here, and here, so there will be no mistake,' he muttered.

He had his hands deep in his coat pockets and, although he was wearing gloves, his fingers were numb, and he would have found that they were useless if he had tried to use them. But he was not aware that they were numb.

A dog barked at him from an alleyway. It was a Yorkshire terrier, lost and confused, and it barked not as a warning but as a plea: *Take me back to my owner.* But Erthmun took no notice of it.

'I climb the tree, you can't catch me,' he muttered. 'Good night, moon,' he muttered. 'Good night, chair.'

A woman came out of a café, saw him – the fixed stare, the quick, stiff gait, hands shoved hard into his coat pockets – and, as he passed close to her, she heard him muttering ('Mother, can we go home, now?'), and stepped away from him. She was a visitor to this city, and Erthmun frightened her. She thought he was just another of the thousands of crazy people she had been told inhabited New York.

And, as she stepped away, Erthmun turned his gaze to her and stopped walking. 'What are you doing?' he asked.

'Nothing,' she answered, her voice high-pitched from fear. 'I'm sorry.'

Erthmun regarded her warily for a few moments. 'You've got to be careful,' he said. 'Don't take people by surprise,' he added curtly, and walked on.

Many decades earlier, in another place

The creature tentatively put his fingers to the wall, as if the wall might be hot, or cold, or as if it might be an enemy. This was the first time he had entered one of the houses, and he sensed hostility – a kind of deep and unnatural tension.

He found that the wall was warm, smooth and hard. Like live skin over flat bone. He disliked the feel of it and he pulled his hand away.

He moved slowly about the dark room, his gaze passing quickly and uncomprehendingly from here to there.

Like the walls, the room itself and its furnishings made him feel strangely out of place and, suddenly, his usually slow, deep and even breathing became erratic, as if the air were being forced from his lungs, as if, somehow, the house itself wanted to take his life from him.

And then – although he was unable to verbalize it – he knew that, in this house, within these walls, he was the enemy. Because he had sensed the other living things in the house, had sensed their fear quivering deep inside them, the way a rabbit quivers deep in its warren.

That fear gave the creature incredible strength

and courage. It excited him, made his muscles tense.

He stopped briefly at the bottom of the stairway.

And something that might, in a human being, have passed for longing or hunger settled into his huge, exquisite, sky-blue eyes.

And then he started up the stairs.

Eleven

When Erthmun woke the following morning, he remembered that he had gone out, but not why or to where. He remembered *being* out, in the night. But he remembered it in the way that other people remember dreams – it was like trying to hold on to a butterfly made of smoke.

When the phone rang, he knew before answering that it would be his lieutenant and that he'd tell Erthmun there had been yet another murder, though Erthmun realized that he had no rational way of knowing all this.

The lieutenant said, 'Internal Affairs isn't suspending its investigation, Jack, but we really do need you down there,' and he gave Erthmun the location of the latest murder – an apartment building on 82nd Street. Erthmun was at the building a half-hour later.

Patricia David, dressed well and wearing a trendy

brown hat, was waiting for him inside the front door. She smiled unsteadily and said, 'We're calling these the "Chocolate Murders".' She looked a little queasy. 'Brief, descriptive, catchy,' she added. 'It'll play well at the *Post*.'

'Uh—' said Erthmun, who had wanted to say *uh-huh*, but couldn't because of the smell here – once more, the overpowering smell of sweet, cheap chocolate – and the body, female, mid twenties, awash in its own blood, except for the white and pretty face, eyes as transparently green as the leaves of an air fern.

'Again, contacts,' Patricia said.

'Uhn—' said Erthmun, who was bending over the body and looking into its eyes. 'This is not a coincidence,' he said, without turning away from the body. 'The killer puts these contacts in.'

'That's very odd,' Patricia said.

'Odd,' said Erthmun. 'Everything's odd.'

'Nothing like it, ever. We've checked,' said Patricia. 'How do you know the killer puts the contacts in?'

'Helen,' said Erthmun.

'Shit,' said Patricia.

He turned and looked at her. 'Did I say "Helen"?'

'You did, yes.'

'Yes. I don't know why. I don't believe this woman's name is Helen.' He was feeling very confused and fuzzy-headed, as if he were in the first moments of an illness.

Patricia said, 'No one knows what her name is, Jack. There's no ID. No clothes anywhere. We assume she lived in the building. We're checking.'

'She does,' Erthmun said.

'You knew her?'

'Knew her? No. How could I?'

'Jack, you're beginning to make no sense.'

'She lived here. That's why she died here. It makes perfect sense.'

Patricia sighed and tried to think of some response.

Erthmun said, 'We are born where we all must die. What could be clearer?'

'Are you kidding, Jack?' She knew that this wasn't likely. Erthmun laughed only occasionally, and he never made jokes. 'Are you making a little joke?'

Her question confused and offended Erthmun. He looked at the body again. He centred on the eyes. He reached, touched one of them.

'For God's sake, Jack,' Patricia said, 'we already know that she's dead.'

'I'm doing nothing,' Erthmun said. 'I'm touching her eyes. I need to touch them.'

'Shit,' said Patricia.

'Shit,' said Erthmun. 'I'm not going to remove the contacts.'

'Don't touch them, Jack. If you're right – for God's sake, if you're right, and the killer put them in, they could contain his fingerprints.'

'They don't.'

She came forward, bent over, took Erthmun's arm. He yanked it away, miscalculated, jabbed his finger hard into the victim's eye, felt the eyeball pop.

'Good Lord,' Patricia said.

'It's nothing,' Erthmun said. 'It's not important.'

'Jack, stand away from the body!' Patricia ordered. He stayed where he was, bent over the body, his gaze on its eyes.

'Jack, I'm telling you to stand away.'

'I can't. How can I?'

'How *can* you? By God, you *will*!'

He looked at her. She had drawn her weapon, though she wasn't pointing it at him; she was holding it at her side. He glanced at the weapon, then into Patricia's eyes, which were the eyes of a cop, then at the popped eye of the victim. He stood abruptly and said, 'I'm sorry. You're right.'

'Step away from the body, Jack!'

He did so. Patricia came forward, put herself between him and the body and called, 'O'Connell, come in here.'

A uniformed cop came in.

She said to him, 'I'm ordering this detective to leave the crime scene. Will you see that he doesn't come back in here?'

The cop nodded once, uncomprehendingly. 'Sure,' he said.

'Jack,' Patricia said, and nodded towards the door.

Erthmun nodded, too, and left with the uniformed cop.

Twelve

Smalley said, 'I've got a transcript of your conversation with Patricia David at the crime scene, Detective. Do you want to read it?'

They were in the interrogation room at the precinct house. Smalley was standing several feet in front of the table where Erthmun was seated. 'Read it?' Erthmun said. 'No, I remember what I said.' In his mind's eye, he saw himself reach far across the table and tear out Smalley's throat. The image was satisfying, and he found himself closing his eyes, found himself *seeing* it happen, *felt* Smalley's blood wash over him, and when he opened his eyes, he discovered that his arm had risen from the table top, and that his fingers were wide. He lowered his arm abruptly, saw that Smalley was looking questioningly at it, and looked away.

After an uneasy silence, Smalley told him, clearly trying for a tone of bravado, 'Of course you remember what you said, Jack.' He came to the table, leaned over it. 'I talked with your sister. She has some very weird ideas about you.'

'Chalk it up to sibling rivalry.'

'For instance, that you've never had a long-term relationship with a woman. Is that true?'

'I've had as many relationships as you have,' Erthmun said.

Smalley straightened, smiled. 'I doubt that, Detective. I really doubt that.' His smile faded. 'But that's not the question I asked, is it? I asked if you have ever had a long-term relationship with a woman.'

'A long-term relationship with a woman,' Erthmun said. 'Listen, am I a suspect in these killings?'

Smalley savoured the moment before answering. 'Yes,' he said, and smiled again. 'As far as I'm concerned, you are.'

'And, as a suspect, am I being removed from active duty?'

'That's up to the captain. I'm recommending that you be put on unpaid leave.'

'Am I going to be arrested?'

Another smile. 'It's likely.'

'On what evidence?'

'There is no direct evidence. You know that. We're talking to you because of your behaviour at these crime scenes. I think you knew these women. Shit, I'm *positive* you knew these women. You could very well be a material witness.'

'Knew these women? Prove it. You can't.'

'Goddammit, you knew them and you killed them. That's what I believe. It's what I *know*!'

Erthmun stood, withdrew his .38, put it on the desk, followed that with his badge. He looked at Smalley, who looked confusedly at the badge and the .38 for a moment, then, just as confusedly, into Erthmun's eyes. 'What's this all about?' he said.

Erthmun left the room without answering.

He got into his bed before dark, while the pale light of late afternoon was on him. He could feel the light on his face. Usually, it was warm, and forgiving, and maternal. Now it wasn't, and he didn't know why.

He was more exhausted than he had ever been. Surely, he thought, it was the kind of exhaustion that was like the quick approach of death, overwhelming and inescapable.

But sleep eluded him. Perhaps because it was still daylight, or because he was simply too exhausted to sleep (a complaint he had heard from others, but which he did not understand).

He lay with his eyes open under his cocoon of blankets. He was stiff and tense, as if expecting some deadly surprise. This made him feel like an animal in hiding from predators. It was a feeling he could not remember having experienced before, and he didn't like it. It made him want to lash out at random noises – the radiators clicking, horns blaring, the rushing noise of the refrigerator springing to life.

After an hour, he threw off his blankets, went to

the window and looked out at the street below. Dusk,
now, and the streetlamps had winked on. People
walked quickly, coat collars turned up, heads down,
shoulders hunched. He guessed that it was cold
beyond his window, and he wondered why he –
naked – didn't feel it. He decided that his tension and
his anger were making him warm.

He saw his dim reflection in the window – the
square face, barrel chest, short, well-muscled thighs,
and his great erection, too, which came to him
whenever he was naked. (This had caused him end-
less trouble when he had found himself naked among
other men, because erections equalled arousal, of
course, and if he was with other naked men, then,
ipso facto, it was they who were causing his arousal.
But this was not so, and he had tried, as a teenager,
to convince other young men that it wasn't so. 'I'm
simply . . . *ready*!' he declared, which was the truth,
as he saw it, but it elicited gales of hooting laughter.)
His reflection started a moment's impulse to violence,
as it usually did, but the impulse dissipated almost at
once.

This night no one looked up at him as he stood
naked at his window. New Yorkers did not usually
look up as they walked. They held their heads at a
slightly downward angle and walked quickly, with
purpose; it was a statement to any who might want
to bother them – *Don't bother me*!

But Erthmun wasn't interested in his nakedness at
his window, and he wasn't interested in the briskly

moving passers-by four storeys below, or in the glowering Manhattan sky. He was interested in the creature who had come to live in his city. The creature who killed with sweet and sick gusto, and who left her victims looking foolish.

She was there, in the night, where he was so unwilling to follow. She was there, in those buildings, with those people. She joked with them and laughed with them and slept with them. But she was not one with them.

She was one with *him*.

He lurched away from the window, suddenly, as if he had been dealt a physical blow.

One with him? One with him? What was he thinking? He didn't even know her name. He had never seen her. He wasn't even certain that she *was* a she.

He sat on his bed, bent forward, cupped his hands on either side of his face.

He knew *her*.

She was murderous and predatory, and she lived only to bring herself pleasure, and others pain.

And she came from the same place that he had come from.

Thirteen

Many decades earlier, in another place

Even as she struggled out of sleep, the woman knew the source of the acrid smell that filled her nostrils. She nudged her husband, asleep beside her. 'Paul,' she said aloud. 'Wake up!'

'It's too cold,' he groaned.

She shook him. 'Paul, wake up, dammit!'

He opened his eyes, raised his head a little. 'What's wrong? What's that smell?' He sat up suddenly. 'My God . . .' He swung his feet to the floor, stood, grabbed the doorknob tightly, yanked his hand back. He cursed.

His wife scrambled out of bed.

'The doorknob's hot,' Paul said. His voice was trembling. 'It's the house. It's on fire!'

'No,' his wife said firmly. 'It can't be.'

And they both saw the band of flickering yellow light beneath the door.

Paul ran to the window, opened its lock, pushed up. The window refused to budge.

He glanced around. 'Rachel, the washbasin. On the dresser. Quick! Give it to me!'

Rachel grabbed the washbasin. 'I don't understand,' she said as she crossed the room. 'We put the fire out. Why do you want this?' She gave him the washbasin. 'I don't understand. Please, Paul . . .' She turned. 'I don't understand.' She crossed to the door, put her hand on the doorknob. 'Why don't we just—'

'Rachel, no!' Paul shouted.

She let go of the doorknob. She stepped back. Her body shook.

'Don't open that door, Rachel!' Paul ordered.

'Yes,' she murmured. 'Yes, I'm sorry.'

Paul brought his arm back, washbasin in hand, to break the window.

Rachel turned, faced him. 'They did this, Paul. They want us to stay here.'

Paul brought his arm forward. 'No,' he whispered. He stopped its movement half-way to the window. 'No!' he screamed. 'No, you won't, you can't. I won't let you. She's not yours!'

He crossed the room.

He threw open the door.

And in the second before the fire swept over her, Rachel saw the three small perfect faces, and the exquisite sky-blue eyes beyond the window.

And she understood.

The following morning
The child, one of several, is intrigued by the gleaming, bulbous thing in the ashes. He reaches for it. A girl nearby reaches at the same time. 'I don't understand,' she says. 'I don't understand.' The boy, screeching, lashes out at her. She moves off, grunting.

The boy picks up the bulbous thing and turns it around and around, studying it. He puts it into his mouth, tests it with his tongue, bites it, throws it to the ground, and continues searching.

One of the girls lifts a soot-blackened jar from the ashes. She studies it hopefully. Finally, she tosses it to one side. It shatters against the dark bulk of a stove. Soon, a pungent odour wafts to her through the chill air and she turns quickly and moves over to the remains of the jar. Then the other children are upon her, variously tearing at her, trying to push her away, and tearing at the stuff from within the jar. Soon there is no trace of it. And the children continue searching.

No longer are their bellies constantly full. Or their skins warm. No longer have they time for desire.

And so they poke through the ashes.

And tear fitfully at the one to find the bones.

While, around them, the frigid morning collects itself. A December morning. Quiet. But with promise.

In time, there will be no more bones.

And winter is upon them.

Fourteen

'Is he a blood relation?' Mark Smalley asked Lila Grant.

'Is the answer to that question germane to your investigation?' she shot back.

Smalley shrugged, grinned. 'Sure, it's germane.'

'I don't see how.'

'Can't you simply give me a straight answer?'

'Yes, certainly.'

'Can I assume, then, that he is *not* a blood relation?'

'You may assume whatever you like, Mr Smalley. I am obviously not in control of your assumptions.' Her smile was comely and confrontational at the same time.

Smalley's grin became a smirk. 'I should tell you that your responses reveal more than you might believe.'

'I doubt that I am so open a book, Mr Smalley, that

you can say from one moment to the next what I might or might not believe.' She was still smiling. She had a cup of tea in front of her on a coffee table. She picked it up, brought it to her lips, tipped it very slightly – not enough, Smalley guessed, to drink – then put it down.

He was seated opposite her on the uncomfortable Queen Anne settee. He had perched himself on the edge, as if ready to leap from it at any second. He thought that it put people on edge if he looked like he was going to leap up at any second. It was one of several poses he employed. Sometimes, depending upon the person he was talking to, he chose to look relaxed. This, he guessed, lulled the person into believing that he was a friend, or a confidant. But he had sensed that Lila Grant was smart – nearly as smart as he was – and that such a pose wouldn't work. It was best, with smart people, to appeal to their fear and paranoia, to play with their emotions. This dulled their intelligence and caused them to slip up.

He said, 'Your brother looks nothing like you, Mrs Grant. There seems to be absolutely no family resemblance. So my assumption is—'

'Again, Detective, your assumptions are of little consequence. Jack is indeed my brother, and I am his sister, and we do indeed share the same mother . . .' she hesitated 'and father. Now if that is the extent of your inquiry—'

'No, of course it isn't!' He heard the tremor in his

voice and it surprised him. He shook his head. 'It's not nearly the "extent of my inquiry", Mrs Grant.'

She nodded, gave him another comely and confrontational smile, delicately sipped her tea again. He looked into her cup as she set it on the coffee table. It was less than half full. He pursed his lips, annoyed, looked at her breasts, saw that she was wearing a bra, looked into her eyes, saw that she was amused.

He leaped from the settee. 'Goddammit, you have simply *got* to be more co-operative with me!'

She smiled up at him. 'When we were children, Mr Smalley, I remember that Jack often volunteered to wash the dishes, especially in the winter. He never told me why he did this, but I guessed that he did it because the hot water felt good on his hands.'

Smalley stared uncomprehendingly at her.

She continued, 'When other children went sledding, Jack stayed inside and read a book, or played a game with our older sister, Sylvia – checkers and Parcheesi were their favourites – or he listened to the radio. He didn't like TV. He's never liked it. He complains that it confuses him. He says that he can actually see the separate scanning lines, and so the picture itself is lost to him.' She shrugged a little, reached for her teacup, touched it, went on, 'It all sounds very fanciful, doesn't it?' She picked up the teacup, with the saucer, held it near her chin, and continued, 'But in summer, and spring, and in the autumn, you couldn't keep him in the house. He'd stay out for hours and hours. Even in the pouring

rain. Actually, he loved the rain. I don't believe that
he loves it quite so much now.' She smiled ruefully.
'I suppose that's all a regrettable part of growing up.'
She sipped her tea; it made a slurping noise as it
passed her lips, which jarred Smalley. She set down
the cup. 'So you see, we really did grow up together.
I know him as well as anyone. He's my brother, after
all.'

She was watching a movie in a theatre on 42nd
Street. The movie was a sweeping, romantic saga
laced with violence and lust, pain and forgiveness,
heartache, death and renewal. She loved it. It spoke
to her. It was a romance of the earth, a story about
people who tilled the land and created children, who
built dynasties and amassed great wealth and power,
who sought to make of themselves, at any cost,
something that the world would long remember. The
movie's message was, *We are far more important than
that which has created us!* It was a message with which
she rabidly agreed. Isn't a great work of art far greater,
she maintained, than the artist who creates it? And
wasn't *she* a work of art? Wasn't she the earth's
masterpiece? Wasn't she something unique, and fantastic? Wasn't she the only true predator in a world
of prey?

Erthmun opened his apartment door and saw a cat in
the long hallway. It sat facing him, and its large eyes

were on him. It was licking its chops, as if it had just eaten something tasty. It was a big, grey cat, and Erthmun could hear it purring, even though it was at the end of the long hallway. *Big cat, big purr*, Erthmun thought.

A door opened near the cat and a young woman dressed in a blue satin robe came part-way into the hall, bent over, and scooped up the cat. As she straightened, she saw Erthmun and nodded and smiled at him. He nodded back.

'Hello, Mr Erthmun,' she said.

'Hello,' he said. He looked quickly down at himself, uncertain that he wasn't naked. He saw that he, too, was wearing a blue robe.

The woman said, 'We're both wearing blue robes.'

Erthmun nodded. He felt an erection starting. The woman was tall, brunette, and her mouth went a little crooked when she smiled, as if she were remembering some delicious secret. Erthmun said, referring to their blue robes, 'We are, aren't we.'

She nodded. She stroked the cat's ears as they talked. The animal's purring was very loud. It was so large that its rear end hung to below her waist, and its tail to her knees. Erthmun didn't believe that he had ever before seen such a large cat.

He said, 'That's an awfully big cat.'

'He's a Maine coon cat,' said the young woman, and gave Erthmun one of her crooked smiles. He loved this smile – it fired up his erection.

He saw her glance at his crotch; she smiled once more. 'It was good talking to you, Mr Erthmun,' she said. 'Perhaps we can talk again.'

'Talk again,' Erthmun said. 'Yes.' But she had already disappeared into her apartment.

In his own apartment, Erthmun thought about mounting the woman in the blue robe. She could even hold her big cat while he did it, he decided. He would bend her over the bed and mount her from behind. He'd lift up her robe and enter her while she cradled her cat in her arms. She would smile her crooked smile, and her big cat would purr while Erthmun pushed himself into her. He'd put his hands on her ass while he pushed into her, and he'd knead one cheek of her ass while she smiled her crooked smile.

He ejaculated as these thoughts came to him. And when his erection subsided, and as the pleasure of his ejaculation slowly left him, he looked down at his stained blue robe, and he felt suddenly, completely and terribly alone.

Patricia David stared at the body splayed out in the bottom of the empty dumpster on East 75th Street and said to the detective with her – a heavy-set, jowly and, as legend had it, deadly serious middle-aged man named McBride – 'This is a copycat killing.'

'Is it?' said McBride. 'How can you tell?'

'Look at the wounds.' She played her flashlight

along the length of the naked body. 'It's like someone went after her with a lawnmower, for Christ's sake. There's no finesse here.'

McBride harrumphed his agreement.

'This is not a good thing,' Patricia said.

'It's a terrible thing,' said McBride.

'I mean that we have a copycat killer,' Patricia said. 'One killer was awful, but two is really lousy.'

McBride gave her a disapproving look.

'You don't agree?' Patricia said.

'With what?'

'That two killers is really lousy.'

'I don't think "lousy" is the word I'd use under these circumstances.'

'Oh,' Patricia said.

'I think "tragic" is more the word I'd use.'

'Sure, it fits.'

'This young woman' – he nodded at the corpse – 'was someone's daughter, someone's sweetheart, someone's mother, perhaps.'

'Conceded.'

'And she has been reduced to . . . this.' He looked at the body. 'You know, she looks like . . . her face looks like the face of a girl I took to a dance once. I think it was a dance. It might have been a movie.' He glanced confusedly at Patricia, then at the body again. 'I think it *was* a movie. *Breakheart Pass*, I think. With Charles Bronson.' He glanced at Patricia again, held out his hand for the flashlight; she gave it to him. He shone the light on the corpse's face. 'Jesus, she's the spit and image of that girl. Her name was Brenda. Pretty little thing.' He held the light on the corpse's face for a long while without speaking.

'And?' Patricia said.

'And not a whole hell of a lot,' said McBride. 'This isn't Brenda. It couldn't be. Brenda's my age, now.'

'Of course,' said Patricia.

'But she could be Brenda's daughter. I don't think she is Brenda's daughter, of course. But she could be.' He shone the flashlight down the length of the body. 'Jees, I hate to see this sort of thing. Don't you hate to see this sort of thing? It's so . . . disrespectful.'

'At the very least,' said Patricia.

'I mean, she could be somebody's *mother*, for God's sake. Or somebody's sister.'

'Yes. It's possible.'

'And now here she is. In a dumpster! No one deserves to end up in a dumpster, wouldn't you agree?'

Patricia said nothing. She guessed that his question was rhetorical.

He looked at her. 'Well, don't you?'

She nodded quickly. 'Yes. I agree. It's a horrible place to end up.'

'Damn right. I mean, it's not like she's a transient or something. Good Lord, she could be somebody's *mother*.'

Fifteen

The man thought, *I am powerful, and I am in control.*

He had photographs. He had developed them in a rented darkroom, and they were spread out in front of him on his kitchen table.

He lived in one room and shared a bathroom with nine other tenants on the second floor of his building. The building was on 123rd Street, and it was rambling, nasty and decrepit.

The man thought he was a very good photographer. He had used his new flash attachment well; he had illuminated the woman's body without causing harsh reflections and without making her loom out of the dark background like a phantom. He had many talents and photography was only one of them.

Murder, he guessed, was another. This first ambitious effort, at any rate, indicated that he had much potential. And it was unfortunate that the *Post* referred to him as a 'copycat'. When a man embarks on a new endeavour, he has to start somewhere. Why not on a path that has led another to glory? Later, he could make his own path.

He loved his photographs. They were the best he'd ever done because they were *real*. No poses, no artifice. Just reality, hard, cold and pungent!

A knock came at the door and he snapped his gaze to it. No one had ever knocked at his door. He paid his rent on time and stayed away from the others who lived in the building, so who could be knocking? Certainly not the police. He was too smart for them. And they wouldn't knock anyway.

Another knock – soft, but insistent.

'Who's there?' he called.

'Who's there, indeed?' he heard. It was a woman's voice.

This was wonderful. Fortuitous. Karmic. A woman at his door!

He stood, glanced at his photographs, thought briefly of hiding them, decided that the woman at his door would be impressed with them, went to the door, opened it quickly.

She was beautiful. Beyond beautiful. Sky-blue eyes and hip-length auburn hair and a body that was the promise of pleasure. 'Do you know me?' she said.

'No,' he said, grinning obscenely. 'Not the way I'd like to.'

'And you are?'

'Roger,' he said.

'Well, then, Roger,' she said, and moved past him into his room, 'I have something for you.'

He watched her move, loved the way she moved, thought she would look good to his lens, and to his weapon, and then to his bawdy instrument.

She was turned away from him. She was perfectly configured, he thought. Perfectly wrought and conceived. He said, 'Oh, what?'

And she turned as quickly as a snake and plunged her hand deep into his gut, into his colon, and snarled, 'Oblivion, asshole!'

Sixteen

**Thirty-eight years earlier: August in the
Adirondack Mountains, near the house on Four
Mile Creek**

This is good here, the woman thought in so many
words. She was inclined to such thoughts. She was a
poet, and her work had been published in several
university journals and small literary reviews. She
had even had a nibble of interest from a New York
City book publisher, although she had been giving
the idea of book publication more than a few second
thoughts because she wasn't sure that she was quite
ready. She did not believe that her work was yet
mannered enough. It tended, as well, towards the
darkly romantic, and it was filled with unfortunate
angst, worry and despair. She needed to cultivate a
lighter attitude, although poetry, she maintained,
should not be about love, it should be about hope,

which was so much more than love. It was more than
sex, too, of course, which was, itself, so much less
than love or hope.

She smiled as these thoughts came to her on this
warm and sunlit afternoon. Smiled because she could
not remember having had such fanciful thoughts –
perhaps she could work them into a poem before
long. Smiled, too, because the birds were gaily chat-
tering at her, and because the squirrels were gambol-
ling playfully in the oaks and tulip trees, and because
the honeybees were busily foraging among the
wildflowers.

It was surely a poet's day!

She was happy that no one else was about. Happy
that Thomas had found this secluded place for them
to raise their three young daughters. As a family, they
could choose when to engage in social relationships,
and they could choose when to enjoy solitude, which
was what she had chosen for herself today.

She thought that she would like to lie down in the
tall pale green grass. It was something she had never
done before, though she had seen it depicted in
paintings. She had always been a little leery of doing
it herself because meadows such as this were alive
with insects and spiders. But she thought that that
should be of no consequence to her. Insects and
spiders were, after all, a part of the natural and
benevolent world to which Thomas had brought her
and the children. He might not be a kind and benevolent man himself, but Thomas Erthmun was

thoughtful enough to put his wife and daughters in a kind and benevolent place.

Out of the corner of her eye, she saw movement in a line of trees not far off, as if someone were running. She turned her head quickly, but saw nothing. Who could be here? It was miles to another house and, besides, their land was posted. Perhaps she had seen a deer, or a fox. Yes, of course. There was no doubt of it. She had seen a deer or a fox. It made her glad, and she smiled again.

But she did not lie down in the grass right away. She kept her eyes on the line of trees where she had seen movement until, at last, a chipmunk appeared on the side of a great oak and she sighed and thought, *Well that's what I saw. A chipmunk.* And she lay down in the tall grass, adjusted herself so that her head was comfortably on a clump of earth, spread her arms wide, closed her eyes, and let the warm sunlight play on her face. This was wonderful, she thought. This was heaven. Alone with the works of nature. Alone with what God had wrought. Somewhere in this experience there was a poem.

She heard movement in the grass nearby. Her eyes popped open. She thought of calling out, 'Who's there?' But she kept silence. Who could be there? Who would disturb this perfect and poetic moment, these minutes stolen from eternity, this time that she had given her soul to breathe? But, still, she turned her head a little so that she was looking in the direction where she had heard movement. She saw the tops of oak and tulip trees, a coagulated mass of pale green grasses, a praying mantis moving on the earth close to her face. She listened. After a minute, she closed her eyes again, let the sunlight play on her skin and let her soul breathe.

She was dressed well, in a long, flowing, earth-coloured skirt and a long-sleeved green cotton blouse that had no pockets, and which billowed nicely around her breasts and hugged her waist. Her hair was red, and she wore it long. Thomas had told her often that she was an attractive woman, and she knew that it was true, but she did not want to cultivate this attractiveness because it was superficial.

Sleep had never come to her with difficulty. It did not come with difficulty now. The sun was warm, a leisurely breeze was stirring the tall pale green grasses, and she was alone in the meadow, except for her soul, which could soar on the wings of this glorious day.

So she slept.

And she dreamed.

And, in her dream, she saw the face of an angel above her. It was a dark and perfect face, and its eyes were sky-blue, and enormous passion was in its mouth.

And then she felt her own passion responding, felt it swelling up from within her, heard the moans that came from her own mouth, and felt, too quickly, too quickly, the inrush of seed and love and man.

And she awoke breathing very hard, and saw that

her earth-coloured skirt was around her waist, and that her panties were torn, and her legs wide, and that the insides of her thighs were chafed and wet. And she heard something moving off swiftly through the sunlit weeds.

And when she turned her head to look, she saw flowing dark hair and a naked back and a naked ass.

And she screamed.

Seventeen

Patricia David had never visited Erthmun at his apartment in the West Village. She had never needed to – she'd always assumed that their relationship was strictly professional. She had suspected, in fact, that she didn't like him very much. She respected him as a cop, but he was often humourless, distant, offputting, at times even rude. He was clearly a man who valued his privacy, and she had always been more than happy to give it to him.

So she was a little perplexed as to why she was ringing his buzzer and waiting for some response from him through the building's intercom. She could have telephoned. She had no reason to believe – now that their professional relationship had been put on hold – that he needed to see her any more than she thought she needed to see him.

She rang the buzzer for a third time. Shit, it was

obvious that he wasn't home. She reached behind her, found the knob for the outside door.

'Yes?' she heard through the intercom.

She hesitated, let go of the knob, pressed the talk button. 'Jack?' she said tentatively.

'Yes.'

'It's me. Patricia.'

Silence.

'Jack?'

'I'm here. What is it?'

She sighed.

'I don't know. I was a little . . . concerned—'

'Concerned? Do you want to come up?'

'Not if I'm disturbing you. Am I dis—'

The inner door clicked; she grabbed the knob, opened the door, heard, 'You know the apartment number?'

She stretched her arm back for the talk button and called, 'Yes. It's how I buzzed you in the first place.'

'Oh, of course,' Erthmun said distractedly.

He had wrapped himself in a green quilt to answer his door. She thought that he was shivering a little beneath it, and that he did not look rested or happy. He even seemed to be having trouble keeping his eyes open.

'You were asleep, Jack?' Patricia said from outside the door. 'I'm sorry.' She glanced at her watch, saw that it was barely 8.00 p.m., gave him a look of concern. 'Are you ill?'

He shook his head. 'Ill? No, it's all right.' His voice was hoarse. 'Come in.' He backed away unsteadily from the door.

She looked past him, into the apartment. It was dark, except for light filtering in from the windows. She said, 'Could you turn a light on, Jack?' He nodded and flipped a switch next to the doorway. A low-wattage overhead copper fixture bathed the room in a yellowish light. She saw a threadbare red couch, under the windows, a white enamel dining table and two white wooden chairs, a small refrigerator; a black clock radio stood on top of the refrigerator.

Jack took another step back. 'Are you coming in?' he said. He sounded peeved.

But she thought she wasn't sure if she was coming in. Perhaps this had been a mistake. Jesus, the man lived like a hermit, and from his tone and demeanour, she was the last person he wanted to see tonight.

'Patricia, please,' he coaxed. 'I'm glad you're here.'

'You are?'

He managed a lopsided smile.

She stepped into the apartment. He closed the door. She stood quietly for a moment, then said, 'This is very Spartan, isn't it?'

'It's my taste,' Jack said. He was standing behind her, at the door.

'No TV?' she said, because she was an avid TV watcher. She glanced around at him.

'No TV,' he said, and managed another smile. She thought he was doing more smiling now than he had

ever done during their shifts together. 'Why don't I
put some clothes on, Patricia.' He went to his bed,
where he'd draped a pair of jeans and a grey sweat-
shirt over the footboard; he scooped them up, went
into his little bathroom, and reappeared moments
later. He smiled again; it was a good and comforting
smile, she thought, though she did not feel comforted
by it and wasn't sure why. 'Okay,' he said. 'What can
I do for you?'

She shrugged. 'Nothing, really.' She looked around
for a chair, saw that there was only the threadbare
couch and white wooden dining chairs. She gestured
at them: 'Can I sit down, Jack?'

'Can you sit down?' Another smile; he seemed
amused. 'Why wouldn't I let you sit down, Patricia?'

She shrugged again. She realized how nervous she
looked and it embarrassed her – they'd worked
together for over a year, after all. She nodded, went
to one of the dining chairs, pulled it out, sat on it.

'You could sit on the couch, Patricia,' Erthmun
said.

'No, no. This is good. I've always liked sitting in
kitchens.'

'I don't have a kitchen.'

'Sure, well, this is a kitchen,' she said, meaning the
dining table and chairs, the refrigerator, the little gas
stove.

He sat across the table from her, smiled again his
good and comforting smile, and she thought she was
beginning to feel at least a little comforted by it. 'It's

pleasant to see you, Patricia,' he said. 'I'm glad you came.'

'I should have called first,' she said.

He shook his head. 'Do you want something? Some coffee, a beer, maybe some tea?'

'Thanks, no. I'm not staying long—'

'Why not?'

'Why not?' The question took her aback.

Erthmun said, 'You can stay as long as you'd like.' He reached across the table a bit, as if to touch her hand, though his reach didn't extend far enough. His fingers fluttered for a moment in the air between them, then he laid his hand flat on the white enamel table top.

Patricia lowered her gaze because his was so ... expectant. 'Jack, I'm sorry ... Did you believe that I—'

'Did I hope that you were coming on to me?' Another smile. 'Perhaps.'

She shook her head, gaze still averted. 'I was concerned about you, Jack. Only concerned. And I thought you might like an update.' She heard a little tremor in her voice, as if she were lying; it surprised her.

'An update,' Jack said.

'On these murders.'

He nodded a little. 'On these murders. Yes. I'd like an update.'

She wasn't sure if she believed him. She said: 'Actually, there's not much to report.' Again, she heard a tremor in her voice. 'You know about the copycat—'

'I read the papers.'

'Then you know that he was murdered?'

'Yes.'

She took a breath. 'I probably shouldn't be telling you this, Jack, since you're not involved with the investigation any more . . .' She hesitated as if uncertain how to continue.

'Go on,' Erthmun coaxed.

She nodded stiffly. 'He had the same things done to him that the killer did to the women.'

Erthmun didn't miss a beat. 'You mean the chocolate in the mouth, et cetera?'

Patricia tried to gauge his demeanour; his tone seemed oddly flat. 'Yes,' she said.

He nodded a little, his grey eyes closed as if he were in thought. He said nothing for a long moment:

'Jack?' she said.

He opened his eyes. She saw something indefinable in them – a strange combination of desperation, panic, memory. He said, 'Then his killer was the same person who killed the two women.'

'Yes. The killer was making a statement, I think. Putting the copycat in his place.' She felt a little smile creep onto her lips.

'Putting the copycat in his place.' He paused. 'Yes, that's obvious, isn't it?'

'The green contacts, too,' Patricia said.

'Of course,' Erthmun said. He sounded suddenly disconnected from the conversation.

Patricia pushed on, 'And as for the overall investigation, we have just about zip, I'm afraid. No prints, no weapon—'

Erthmun cut in, 'I would have been glad, Patricia, if you *had* been coming on to me. But since you weren't, and aren't that's okay.' He leaned far over the table and touched her finger.

She looked silently at his hand.

He said, 'Am I making you uncomfortable?'

She lifted her gaze to his and nodded a little.

'Why?' he said.

Why? she wondered. For God's sake, he had to ask why? 'Perhaps this was a mistake, Jack.' She stood.

'It wasn't,' he said. 'Please, sit down. I really have no expectations at all in this situation.'

She thought about this, decided he was sincere, realized that she didn't know what her own expectations were tonight. At last, she sat down again, sighed and said, 'Tell me how Internal Affairs is treating you, Jack.'

'I'd rather not.'

'I understand.'

'It's unpleasant. It's business. They're treating me poorly.'

'Smalley seems like a real asshole,' Patricia said.

'He's a man doing a job,' Erthmun said. He sat back

in his chair, smiled again – clearly to get on to another topic – and said, 'I'm going to have a beer. Have one with me, okay?'

She nodded. 'Sure.'

He stood, went to his refrigerator, poked around in it, came back to the table with two bottles, asked if she needed a glass. 'No,' she said, and he sat across from her again.

He said, 'I want to tell you something significant.'

This made her want to laugh. It was so formal. 'Significant?' she said.

He wrapped his hand tightly around his beer bottle, looked earnestly at her for a moment, then turned his head to look out the window. She noticed, for the first time, an odd smell in the place. It wasn't unpleasant. It was evocative of . . . the earth, she thought, and she realized that she had smelled it before, at other times, while she and Jack had worked together. But it was less distinct, then.

He said, 'I am not the person I appear to be.'

Her immediate inclination was to say, *Who is?* But this would be trite, she decided, even insulting. Clearly, Jack thought that his pronouncement was indeed significant, so she said nothing.

He went on, 'I would say, in other words, that I don't know who I am.'

'Sort of like a mid-life crisis?' Patricia offered.

He grinned and shook his head. 'No. It's too soon for that.'

She grinned back, embarrassed.

'Shit, Patricia, I'm only thirty-seven years old. Do I look older?'

'No, no. You look thirty-seven.'

Another grin. 'Not thirty-five or thirty-eight?'

She chuckled.

He said, 'Do you remember much of your childhood, Patricia?'

'Yes. I had a good childhood. I'm a little surprised when other people complain about their unhappy childhoods. Mine wasn't. Mine was okay. I remember most of it, I think. I remember milking a cow when I was . . . two years old.'

'You grew up on a farm?'

'No. I was a city brat. But my grandparents lived on a farm and we visited them a lot. They were great. They used to sing us French folk songs and my grandfather played caroms with us till our fingers hurt—'

'Caroms?'

'Sure. Caroms. You never played caroms?'

'I don't remember playing any games when I was a kid, Patricia.'

This announcement surprised her. 'All kids play games, Jack. It doesn't matter who they are or who their parents are. All kids play games. The kids in Harlem have the fire hydrants turned on in the summer and they run around in the water. That's a game.'

'I remember running, yes,' Erthmun said. 'I remember running everywhere.' He leaned over the table and lowered his head so that his gaze was on the lip of his beer bottle. 'Jesus, I could run like a fucking jack-rabbit. Jesus!' He grinned. 'I don't *look* like I could run like a jack-rabbit, do I? But I could. I remember it.'

Patricia reached far across the table and touched his hand. She wanted to say something comforting.

He went on, looking at her, 'I had three sisters, did you know that?'

She shook her head. 'No, I didn't.'

He nodded, lowered his gaze again. 'One died shortly after I was born.'

'I'm sorry.'

'She disappeared, actually. She was six years old. She went out to play . . . she went to a place that my mother had told her to stay away from, and no one ever saw her again.' He closed his eyes and shook his head, as if the memory gave him pain, although, Patricia guessed, he couldn't have remembered the incident. 'They found her clothes. Her shorts and her shirt and shoes. Her sneakers, I mean. I remember that my mother told me to stay away from the same place when I was three or four. I don't think I obeyed her. I can't remember. I think I went there once or twice. I think I actually went there looking for my sister. The sister I'd never met.' He glanced out of the window, then into Patricia's eyes again. 'I've seen pictures of her. She was a cute little thing.'

'She looked like you, Jack?'

He shook his head. 'No. Neither of my surviving sisters looks like me. They're all tall and blonde.'

'Very pretty, then.'

'Very.'

She saw her *faux pas*. 'Jees, I didn't mean that the way it sounded, Jack. You're a very attractive man.'

'A very attractive man,' Jack said. 'I'm built like a fire hydrant.'

'Yes, but you're a very attractive fire hydrant. I mean that.'

He nodded, said they were getting off the subject, to which Patricia said, 'I didn't know we were on a particular subject.'

'Yes,' he said. 'We are. Me. Fascinating subject.' Then he smiled again, and she realized, at last, what all his smiling and grinning should have already told her.

'My God, Jack, this *is* some kind of crisis you're going through, isn't it?'

'Crisis?' he said, and seemed to think about the word for a moment. 'Yes,' he said, still smiling.

'I'm talking about a personal crisis,' she said. 'This is a personal crisis for you.'

'It's that and a lot more,' he said. 'And I'm sorry I've trapped you in it.'

'Trapped me in it? I don't feel trapped.'

'But you are, Patricia.'

It sounded like a threat, though Patricia was certain he hadn't meant it that way. She said, 'I don't know

what you mean, Jack,' and felt a nervous grin play
on her mouth. She took a sip of her beer, heard it
pass noisily down her throat, chuckled a little, embarrassed, and set the bottle down hard on the table
top.

Erthmun said, 'Do I scare you?'

'Scare me?' she chirped.

'I do, don't I?'

'No. Why should you?' She gave him a big broad
smile.

'I shouldn't,' he said. 'But I think I do. I'm ...
unpredictable.'

She said nothing. He was right, but she didn't want
to tell him so.

He said, 'I scare myself these days.' He stopped
talking; he looked perplexed.

'And?' Patricia coaxed after a few moments.

'It's like ... Do you know about the tumours some
people get? They get tumours – in their groin, say, or
in their arm pit, and when the doctors take them out,
these tumours are the remnants of that person's twin?
Have you heard of that? Jesus, it's ghastly, isn't it?
Ghastly!'

Patricia didn't know what to say. She took another
noisy sip of her beer. She wanted to leave the apartment, but had no idea how to do it without hurting
his feelings. He was right, she realized. She really *was*
trapped.

He went on, 'It's like I have one of those twins
inside me, Patricia. But it isn't a twin, *per se*. It's not a

clot of foetal matter that might once have been my
brother.' He grinned oddly. 'It's part of *me*.' He
paused, as if for thought, then continued, 'It's what
completes me.' He seemed to think about this, too. He
sighed. He looked hopelessly at sea. 'Do you have any
idea what I'm talking about, Patricia?'

She didn't. She said, 'I think so, Jack. I'm not sure.'
She took another noisy sip of her beer.

'Listen, I'm sorry,' he said. 'This all sounds very,
very strange, doesn't it? I'm really sorry. But there's
something else, too. This thing inside me, this . . . *me*
inside me . . . Jesus, Jesus, it's – ' he pointed stiffly at
the window ' – *out there*, too! And it's not just one, or
two or three, it's . . . dozens.'

She nodded quickly. 'Yes, out there,' she said. 'I
understand.'

He looked hard at her, slowly lowered his arm,
wrapped his hand tightly around his beer bottle. 'This
could have been a romantic evening for us, Patricia,'
he said.

Many decades earlier, in another place
The creature had fallen seventy feet to the bare earth
from the upper branches of an aged honey locust.
The creature had climbed the honey locust for no
other reason than it *could* climb it; and it had fallen
because it knew nothing about old trees and decayed
branches. It knew only about itself – about pain and
cold, and how to protect itself from the cold. And it

knew about heat, and hunger, too, and desire. It knew what the earth said it must know.

The creature did not know that it was dying. Since its birth only weeks before, it had killed, and it had seen death, and it had experienced life. But it could not give names or meanings to anything. Its brain was not set up for clutter.

The fall from the honey locust – which would not have been fatal had the creature jumped instead of fallen wildly out of control – had broken its back. Also a lower rib had pierced its heart. And so it was dying. Very painfully and very slowly.

Its eyes followed the subtly changing patterns of light and shadow all around. That changing pattern was what it had first seen, weeks before, when the earth was done giving it life.

The creature could not weep, nor could it smile. If it were human, it might. But it wasn't. So, blankly, it watched the changing patterns of light and shadow; it experienced the pain.

And, in time, life stopped within it.

For ever.

Eighteen

The bus moved leadenly through the deep new snow. Beyond its windows, the Manhattan streets were white and grey, streaked with flashes of yellow – the city's taxis moving about in the storm with the agility and sure-footedness of rabbits.

The woman who called herself Helen sat rigidly in a seat near the back of the bus, where the bus's heater blew hot air on her legs and feet and warmed her enough that she could breathe.

She wasn't frightened, though she could not move. She was a creature caught up in a battle for survival, because she had chanced into the hands of her killer – the storm, the snow, the bitter cold.

She did not give time to regret or self-recrimination. She felt the awful pain that the frigid night air gave her, but she did not cry out or weep. In her short

time on the earth, she had never cried out or wept
because of pain.

Patricia had got up to leave Erthmun's apartment.
The act surprised her. She didn't believe, rationally,
that she was afraid of the man. He puzzled her, she
thought, but surely he didn't frighten her.

She was half-way to the door when he called,
'Don't go out there, Patricia. Please stay.' If she had
listened only to his words, she would have assumed
it was a sexual invitation. But his intonation seemed
to be one of urgency, as if it were desperately important for her to stay in the apartment with him.

She looked back at him and said, 'Why?'

'Because I want you to stay here. With me.'

'I can't.'

'This isn't a come-on. Do you think it's a come-on?'

'No.'

'No. Yes, you do. Of course you do. What else
would it be? But it isn't. I really do want you to stay.
An hour or two. We'll have something to eat. I'll
make us some food. I have lots of food here. I have
steak, I have some steak. I could cook it. You must be
hungry.'

She stared at him for a few moments and it came
to her what was wrapped up in all this babble. He
was trying to protect her.

The woman who called herself Helen did not try to
understand why this cold night was so different for

her from other cold nights. She did not say to herself, *It's because this is the coldest night of the year*, or *The wind chill factor is low*, or *It's a combination of the wind and the snow and the cold*. These facts meant nothing to her. Her pain meant nothing to her – it was merely an obstacle to overcome.

The bus was empty except for her and the driver, and he was taking it back to the garage because his shift was done. He hadn't yet noticed the woman, but he did now, and he called to her, 'You gotta get off the bus, lady.' He pulled over to the kerb and opened the rear doors.

She said nothing. She didn't look at him. The blast of cold air did not make her wince, but it drove her pain deeper, made her muscles tense. And it started in her an instinct and a capacity and a power that she had used often since coming to this city, though not in a way that could draw much attention to her.

The driver said again, 'You gotta get off the bus, lady.' He looked at her in the rear-view mirror, saw that she wasn't looking back at him, muttered, 'Shit,' thought, *She's drunk, dammit!*, stood and started making his way back to her. 'Come on, lady,' he said. 'Don't make life difficult for the both of us.' He stopped walking. She had looked up at him, had levelled her gaze on him. 'Jesus Christ!' he whispered.

'Jesus Christ!' she whispered, and her voice was *his* voice.

He started backing away from her, tried to keep his eyes on her, but he couldn't because she wasn't there.

Then she *was* there. And then she wasn't. She was a
part of the bus seat, a part of the Bacardi Rum sign
overhead, a part of the dark floor, a part of the rear
window and the blowing snow, the headlights, the
neon, the streetlamps, the wind, and the black sky.
But she was teeth, as well, and sky-blue eyes, breasts,
hips, dark pubic hair. She was a naked phantom, and
she was a living woman, dressed for an evening in
cheap hotels. She was a part of the dark floor and the
neon, the blowing snow and the black sky.

The bus driver fell backwards in his desperation to
get away from her. He muttered little pleading
obscenities at her, saw her coalesce with the air itself,
saw her reappear – teeth and hands and breasts and
pubic hair.

And then she was on him.

Patricia said, 'Jack, does all of this have anything to
do with the woman you called Helen?'

'Helen? Yes,' he answered, 'it does. She exists.
There is at least a Helen.'

She gave him a puzzled look. At least a Helen? she
wondered. She said, 'You know this woman?'

'Know this woman? No. I've never met her. I've
never met any of them.'

Patricia sighed. I've never met any of them? What
was that supposed to mean? Jesus, the man was
falling apart before her eyes. She came back and stood
behind her chair at the white enamel table. 'What in
heaven's name are you talking about, Jack? Is this

all in the nature of ... intuition, premonition, precognition ... You're not making a hell of a lot of sense.'

He looked at her a moment, then out of the window, then at her again, and said, 'I don't know what any of that is, really.' He noticed for the first time that a storm had begun.

Patricia said, 'You mean you don't know the definitions of ...'

He gave her a weary smile. 'Sit down, Patricia.' She hesitated, then did so. He said, 'You can't go anywhere, anyway. Look at it out there.'

She looked, scowled. 'Shit,' she muttered.

'So, you see, you've got to stay.'

'Yes,' she said.

'Yes,' he said. 'I'm glad.'

She ate him. Not all of him. Some of him. The tender parts. His palms, his cheeks, his stomach, his thighs. He was an overweight man, and the fat did her good. It gave her warmth, and strength.

And so she left the bus through the rear doors that he had opened for her, and she moved quickly through the snow-covered streets. No one saw her, and no one looked. Few were out and about on the streets of Manhattan this winter night, except the taxis, and if their drivers had passengers then the vision of those drivers was restricted to what lay ahead. If they had looked in her direction, they would have seen only a change in the pattern of the blowing snow, little else, and they would have thought nothing of it.

'Can I have another beer?' Patricia asked. 'If I'm staying, there's no real reason to remain sober.'

Erthmun said, 'I don't really know what that means,' and smiled, got up, got another beer from the refrigerator, brought it back to her. She looked at the label, told him he had good taste in beer.

'I like beer,' he said. 'I like to *eat*, in fact.'

Patricia said, 'You mentioned something about a steak.' She was beginning to feel more comfortable with him. Maybe it was the alcohol, though she didn't make much of an effort to analyse it. She trusted her instincts, though they had been running in different directions this night.

He nodded, went back to the refrigerator, withdrew two T-bones, took them to his little counter, and turned his gas broiler on to preheat. He said, as he took the steaks from their Styrofoam containers, 'I'm hungry, too. I don't usually eat at this time of the night. I'm usually asleep.'

This had not seemed like a rebuke to Patricia, but she said, anyway, 'If I'm keeping you—'

'I'll sleep another night,' he cut in, smiling.

She thought that his smile had changed. There was nothing of crisis in it, now. It seemed to signal that he was genuinely pleased to have her there with him, and this made her feel good.

She stood, joined him at the counter, said, 'Is there something I can do?'

'Do?' he said. 'Yes, you can eat what I make for you.'

'I will,' she said. Then, 'Tell me what you meant about Helen.'

'I don't know what I meant. It was a hunch, I think.' He got a bottle of seasoning from a drawer. 'Do you want some of this on yours?'

'No. I like it plain. And rare.'

'A woman after my own heart.'

'About Helen?' Patricia said.

'About Helen? Not much. I don't know.' He looked oddly at her. 'What's in a name, after all?'

The woman loved being a part of this city. She loved the buildings and the lights and the odour of diesel fuel. During the summer – her first summer – she had loved going into the parks at night and stripping down and running, and running, and running. She loved running at night through the streets, weaving like a quirky breeze through the little knots of people, and then tossing her strange, coarse laughter back at them.

Memories meant little to her, now. She remembered the name she had taken because she loved the sound of it, and she remembered the building where she spent her days, because it was a place where no one else spent time, and so it was a place of protection. And she remembered her birth, especially, because it was a time of enormous pain and incredible pleasure.

And she remembered coming here, to this city. Remembered being drawn to it by the heady mixture of smells, by the noise, by the feel of the air and the ever-present promise of pleasure.

She slept now. She was a night hunter, her hunting was done, and so it was time to sleep. The sounds and smells of the city were distant in this place, distant enough, at least, that they did not draw her. And this early morning, the sounds of the storm covered them, too.

She curled up in her cocoon of quilts and blankets, and she dreamed only of being a clump of earth, a rock, a root. She did not remember these dreams because such things as clumps of earth, rocks and roots simply have no memory.

Nineteen

**Thirty-eight years earlier, summer in the
Adirondacks**

Cecile Erthmun had the words ready, and she could
see that Thomas – who had just come out of the
bathroom and was rubbing his face with a black towel
– was looking expectantly at her, as if he knew she
had something to say, but the words that came out of
her were not the words she so needed to say: 'Bacon
this morning, Thomas?' she said.

He looked silently at her a moment, as if trying to
decide if she was being somehow dishonest, then he
nodded, and went back into the bathroom.

She threw off her blanket, swung her feet to the
floor, heard herself call out, *Thomas, I was raped!* But
she knew that she had said nothing.

She stood.

Thomas reappeared. He was a tall man; his face was

angular and his eyes intense and authoritarian. He went to a closet, opened it, rummaged in it, found a white shirt, put it on. As he buttoned it, he said, 'I'm going to be gone for two weeks, Cecile.'

'Two weeks?' The idea frightened her – herself and the girls alone at the house for two weeks! How could she allow it? 'That long?' she said.

He nodded again. 'Breakfast?' he coaxed.

She nodded back, but stayed where she was, seated on the edge of the bed in her yellow floor-length cotton nightgown. He gave her a questioning smile. She looked away briefly, looked back, smiled a little, stood.

'Is something wrong?' he asked.

She didn't answer at once. She went around the bed, found her slippers, put them on.

'Cecile, I asked you a question.'

She went to a clothes tree near the bedroom door, got her green robe, put it on, looked back at him, sighed and nodded.

He said, 'Is that a yes?'

She nodded again. 'I think . . .' She paused. 'I had some . . . difficulty yesterday, Thomas.'

'Did you?' His tone betrayed no concern.

She nodded. 'Thomas, I think that we should . . . leave here.'

'Leave here? Leave this house?' He was clearly astonished.

She nodded a little, in pretended uncertainty.

'Why in heaven's name should we leave? I have no intention of leaving.'

She heard herself yell at him, *For God's sake, Thomas, I was raped!*

He repeated, 'I have no intention of leaving this house, Cecile. I brought you and the girls here for a reason. The cities are turning into muck and mire. We have had this discussion. Why should I leave this house?'

She stared at him. He was so intransigent. Why had she married him?

He said, 'Home schooling is best for the girls, as we have agreed. And you can write your poetry here. I can think of nothing more fitting for a woman such as you than to be ensconced in her country house writing poetry. It's fitting that this is something a woman should do. And we need have no worry about the filth of the cities infecting us.'

I was raped! she heard herself whisper, and wondered if the words had actually passed her lips.

'What was that?' Thomas said.

She thought that he had heard her say something, and that he was asking her to repeat it. She shook her head. 'Nothing,' she said.

'More than *nothing*,' he said, and moved quickly past her, into the hall. She saw him look left, right. 'Dammit,' he whispered. He looked back into the bedroom. 'Well, didn't you see it?' he snapped.

'See what?'

'Someone ran past this doorway.'

'One of the girls—'

'Not one of the girls! It was male.'

'My God!' Cecile breathed.

Thomas went to the railing that looked out on the first floor of the house.

'Thomas?' Cecile said.

He waved his hand behind him to tell her to keep quiet. 'Quiet. I'm listening.'

'To what?'

'Shut up, Cecile!'

She fell silent.

The house had been built so its façade faced east, and the rising sun. A huge open area stood at the front; a tall, multi-paned window had been built above the door. It was not quite 6.15, and the sun was rising, now, casting yellow light through the tall window and into the house, onto the landing where Thomas stood. A stationary horizontal shadow was also cast through the window; this was a limb of a huge oak tree just inside the perimeter of the stylized picket fence.

As Thomas stood at the landing, a shadow moved on top of the horizontal shadow. 'Oh, yes,' Thomas whispered.

'What is it?' Cecile said.

'The cat,' Thomas said, and turned to face her. 'See there?' He pointed. Part of the shadow of a cat moving on the limb was on the floor of the landing, and on the railing. 'It was the cat,' Thomas repeated.

Cecile shook her head quickly.

'But it was,' Thomas assured her. 'It was the cat.'

It wasn't the fucking cat! Cecile heard herself say.

'Mystery solved,' Thomas said. 'No mystery whatever.' He looked questioning at her. 'Breakfast?' he said.

Twenty

Patricia David thought that her night with Jack Erthmun had been incredible. She thought that she was a reasonably attractive woman – she exercised, usually ate the right foods, wore nice clothes, kept up with current events. Men were *attracted* to her, for Christ's sake. She got asked out by strangers at least three or four times a week. So why in the hell had Jack Erthmun let her sleep on his bed – while he slept on the couch – without making a move? What had the evening meant? It had been clear that he was attracted to her, and she had to admit, however reluctantly, that she was attracted to him.

Her new partner, McBride, apparently caught on to her perplexity because he said from his desk, 'Something wrong?'

She had just come into the squad room; she was forty-five minutes late. She shook her head too quickly. 'No. Nothing.' She heard the peevish tone in her voice and hoped that McBride hadn't heard it, too. She didn't want him asking a lot of questions.

He shrugged. 'Okay.' He handed a Polaroid snapshot across the desk. 'I hope you haven't eaten yet.'

She took the photograph. Her stomach lurched. 'Jesus,' she said, 'this guy looks like he's been *cannibalized!*'

'He was,' said McBride. 'They found him early this morning. He was a bus driver. They found him in his bus.'

Patricia said, staring open-mouthed at the Polaroid, 'You mean, someone actually *ate* him?'

McBride nodded. 'Not all of him, though. Just the juicy parts. His hands, you know. The fleshy parts of his hands, and his gut. His genitals, too.'

'Yes,' said Patricia. 'I see.'

'It's not without precedent, of course. Even in this country. People get eaten a lot more than you might like to think, and I'm not talking only about Jeffrey Dahmer. Sometimes we pull transients and homeless people out of some of these abandoned buildings and you'd swear that it wasn't only rats that had been eating them. Of course, no one looks too closely into these deaths. I mean, who cares, right?'

Patricia didn't answer. She handed back the Polaroid. 'I assume he's at the morgue.'

McBride nodded.

Twenty-one

Thirty-six years earlier, in the house on Four Mile Creek

This is how Cecile Erthmun wanted to begin her admonition to her six-year-old daughter, Rebecca: 'If I've told you once, I've told you a *thousand* times . . .' But she didn't say that because her mother had said the same thing to her, again and again, and she was not about to repeat her mother's mistakes, she was not about to *become* her mother.

Rebecca looked expectantly at Cecile Erthmun. Rebecca was a child who could guilelessly defuse anger with such a look; it was a look that said, *I am listening to you because you love me, and because I love you*.

Cecile Erthmun asked, 'Do you remember what I said about that place?'

Rebecca nodded, her pretty rosebud mouth open a

little, as if she did not really understand the purpose of her mother's question, and her grey eyes locked on her mother's dark brown eyes, because they were, of course, the source of all caring.

'Good, then,' said Cecile Erthmun. 'Good.' She leaned over and gave her daughter a hug. Rebecca very much enjoyed these hugs because her mother smelled of freshly washed clothes and sweet perspiration. Cecile sat on her haunches, took her daughter by the shoulders, and added, 'So you know that it is not a good place to play?'

Rebecca nodded a little, as if unconvinced.

'And you're going to stay right here. In the yard. Isn't that right?'

Another slight nod. 'Yes.'

Cecile hugged her again. 'I know you are, sweetheart,' she said as she hugged. She heard the infant Jack crying from the other room. 'I've got to see to your brother, now. I'm sure one of your sisters will be out to play with you as soon as they're done with their chores.'

Rebecca did not respond to this. It wasn't awfully important to her that her sisters come out and play. Their games weren't very much fun – hide and seek around the tall bushes that were everywhere near the house, leap-frog (which she wasn't big enough for), Simon Says, and tree-climbing, sometimes (though she wasn't big enough for that, either).

But she had other playmates. And they were quicker, and smarter, and they knew lots of tricks.

They could run as fast as birds could fly, and they could say things to her sweetly, the way her mama did, or angrily, like her father, and they could giggle like her sisters, and disappear, *poof*! too, she'd seen it!

And they were everywhere. Not just in the place her mother had told her to stay away from. They were in the trees that her sisters climbed, and in the bushes where her sisters played hide and seek, and around the yard where they played Simon Says, and they were in the house, too.

They were everywhere!

They were wonderful!

Twenty-two

He asked his reflection, 'What in hell is this? Who in the hell are you?' He saw his lips form the words, and heard the words come back to him from the enamel and the glass, from the hard, white plaster walls and the grey tile floor.

He told himself that he was being foolish. He said to his reflection, 'You're a fool.' He saw the lips move, and heard the words come back to him from all the hard surfaces in the little room. 'You're a fool,' he said again. He thought that he should be smiling.

It was a small mirror, mounted at head height above the sink, and he was naked. He couldn't see himself completely in the mirror unless he leaned into it and looked down. He did this, and studied his body in the small mirror. It seemed foreshortened. Fat. He thought that his penis had disappeared into the fat below his belly. What was there to look at? A little dark pink nubbin, like the head of a turtle.

He leaned back from the mirror, looked at his face, said, 'My face,' and thought again that he should be smiling. He leaned forward and looked very closely at the eyes reflected in the glass. He could see only eyes. They were brown and black and rimmed by folds of dark pink skin.

He pushed his forehead and the bridge of his nose hard against the glass for a better look. He felt the cold enamel sink on his belly and his penis. He felt the cold mirror against his forehead and the bridge of his nose. He tried to find himself in his irises, but saw nothing in them but darkness.

The pressure against his penis had given him an erection. This made him angry and he shouted an obscenity that came back to him a thousand times from all the hard surfaces in the little room. He felt his hands tighten around the edge of the sink, felt himself push his forehead harder into the mirror, until it cracked, and he could see a half-dozen eyes there. He pushed his forehead into the cracked mirror, until the shards cracked, so that there were a dozen or more eyes looking back at him. The eyes were brown, and rimmed by folds of dark pink skin. These were his eyes, he knew.

His mother was clearly surprised to see him, and her smooth round face lit up with enthusiasm and happiness. For the first time, he noticed that strands of grey had crept into her red hair. It had been too long since he last seen her.

'Jack,' she said, and leaned to hug him.

They did not hug for very long – their hugs had always been brief – and when they stopped, he said, 'I need to talk to you.'

She nodded enthusiastically, said, 'Of course,' led him inside, and sat him down on a massive blue cloth couch. Two cats were sleeping on the back of the couch, and when he sat down they opened their eyes, blinked at him, blinked again, and, together, slunk off; they threw him backward glances full of fear and mistrust as they made their way out of the room and into the kitchen.

His mother sat beside him. She said that he looked skinny and that he clearly had not been feeding himself properly.

'No. I'm not hungry,' he told her.

'When you were a boy,' she said with a smile, 'you were forever hungry.'

'We need to talk,' he said.

'Yes,' she said, 'I can see that.' She stopped smiling and looked concerned.

A long silence followed while she waited politely and respectfully for him to speak. At last he said, 'I don't know what I want to say.'

She told him that of course he knew what he wanted to say.

He said, 'I should come here more often. I'd like to come and see you more often.'

'Would you?' she said.

He nodded vigorously. 'I would, yes.'

'Then why don't you?'

'Work,' he answered at once.

'Of course,' she said. 'I understand.'

He said, 'I didn't know you had cats.'

'I do, yes, I do,' she said. 'I've had them since the summer. You weren't here in the summer, were you, Jackie? I didn't have them the last time you were here. I got them in the summer, and I named them Oriskanie and Powhattan. Those are good names for cats, don't you think?'

'They are, yes,' he said.

'You seem . . . distracted, son,' she said. 'I can tell these things about my children. You especially.'

He said, 'I need some answers, Mom.'

'Yes,' she said, and put her hands comfortingly on his, which were resting on his knees. 'What answers do you need, Jackie?'

He looked at her hands on his. They were not as smooth as her face, and they felt cold against his skin. They were heavily veined and the skin was grey-blue. He thought, looking at them, that the veins were like the branches of an old tree that reaches into the sky. The analogy appealed to him and he supposed that if this were some other day, it would be an analogy he'd share with her, because she'd enjoy it, too.

He said, his gaze still on her hands, and quickly, as if the words had been piling up for years, 'I don't believe that the man I called Father was the man who was my father. I don't think I ever believed it.' He looked into her eyes, saw something like panic in them, and said, 'Tell me if I'm wrong, Mother.'

She looked away quickly, took her hands from his, stood, leaned over the couch, as if to steady herself. He could see that she was shaking. 'Of course he was your father, Jackie,' she said. 'I wasn't a promiscuous woman. Did you think I was promiscuous?'

'Promiscuous? No, I didn't think that.'

'Your father wasn't easy to get along with, but he was the only man I ever slept with. I never slept with any man but him. Why would I? I'm not promiscuous.' She was crying softly now.

He stood, put his hands on her shoulders, and said, 'I'm sorry.'

She shook her head. 'No. I understand.'

'Do you?'

'Of course. You don't even look like your sisters. But that's all . . . genetics. Who knows what's going to pop out of the mix? Who knows? You throw in a little bit of this and a little of . . . that . . .' Her voice was quaking.

He nodded. He wanted desperately to leave, because he knew that he had made her uncomfortable, and because he knew that she was lying. *You're lying*, he heard himself say, then was thankful when he realized he hadn't actually said it.

She asked, 'Was that the answer you wanted,

Jackie?' She attempted a smile that would put an end to the conversation and lead them onto something else.

He nodded, 'Yes. Thank you.'

She touched his hand and told him that she wanted to prepare him some food. He said yes, he'd like that, and added that it had been a long time, too long, since they had eaten together.

But they ate in near silence; this near silence was punctuated by quick, nervous smiles, and an occasional 'This is good,' from him, and, from her, 'Have you been to visit either of your sisters?' to which he shook his head, and made no explanations.

The cats slunk about the scene as if they were used to begging from the table but were wary of the strange man who had come to visit.

When he left, he said to his mother, at the door, 'We should do this more often.'

She said, smiling, 'Yes, we should,' and they hugged each other, very briefly.

That evening, he could not sleep because his uncle Jack's words came back to him again and again.

'It's like this,' Uncle Jack said. 'You can't see them if you're actually *looking* at them. You won't see them that way. That would be too *easy*, wouldn't it? You can only see them if you're *not* looking at them.'

Lila said, 'What do they look like, Uncle Jack?'

'They look like you – ' he touched her nose gently ' – and you – ' he touched Erthmun's nose ' – and you,' Sylvia's nose. He laughed again. 'And some of them even look like me!'

Lila asked, 'And where do they come from, Uncle Jack?'

'Well, Lila,' Uncle Jack said, 'where does *anything* come from?'

'Where does anything come from?' Erthmun said.

'I don't know,' Lila said, clearly perplexed.

'From heaven,' Sylvia offered.

'From heaven,' Erthmun said.

'From *every*where,' Uncle Jack declared, and gave them all his biggest and wisest smile.

'From *every*where,' Erthmun said.

'*Every*where!' Lila said.

Twenty-three

The woman who called herself Helen had gotten invited to a party in a high-rise near Central Park. The man who had invited her was wealthy and he looked upon her as another acquisition. Helen did not understand this, and it would have meant nothing to her if she did. What interested her was being among the people who lived in this city and making herself one of them. This was important to her because she was a social creature and so she needed the companionship of creatures who, in so many ways, were like her.

She was also an almost entirely reactive being. She did not have the capacity or patience for rumination; she did have the capacity, however, to read people and their intentions toward her as quickly as others read street signs. This was a defence mechanism, and it was as well developed in her as in any of her brothers and sisters.

She had also conformed almost completely to the etiquette and demeanour required of her in this gathering. It was an ability which was not the result so much of intelligence as adaptive response. It was almost chameleon-like. She absorbed the way other females at this gathering acted and reacted, then she *became* a kind of amalgam of what she had absorbed. No one noticed that this was what she was doing, of course, though a few at the gathering thought she was a little odd. One woman said quietly to another, 'It's a good thing she's so drop-dead gorgeous,' and the woman to whom she was speaking nodded her agreement, though neither of them could have said, in so many words, what exactly they were talking about.

'Helen, yes,' Helen said to a self-consciously dapper man in his mid-thirties who had come to the gathering alone but did not want to go home alone.

'Like Helen of Troy,' he said, thinking that she would know the reference instantly – *The face that launched a thousand ships!* – and would realize that he had paid her a high compliment.

Helen said, 'Helen of Troy, yes', which sounded to the dapper man only like a slight rephrasing of 'Helen, yes', as if she were merely repeating herself. He mistook this for self-confidence, which he liked in a woman, and pressed on, 'You're one of Martin's angels?' Martin was the man who had invited Helen; 'angels' was a euphemism for the women that Martin made available to his closest friends.

Helen said, 'Martin brought me here,' and sipped her drink. It was a Manhattan and the taste did not appeal to her, but she had seen others at the gathering drinking similar drinks and they had looked as if they were enjoying them, so she was able to conjure up the same look of enjoyment.

She continued, 'I'm an angel of Martin,' and gave the dapper man a coquettish smile. This was unfortunate because coquettish smiles did not mix well with her naturally predatory and overtly sensual appearance, and so her attempt at playfulness came off as archly dishonest, which almost caused the dapper man to go and hunt elsewhere for his evening's conquest. But he decided to stick with Helen because he thought that she really was a knockout, and so what if she was a bit strange?

'Have you known him long?' the dapper man asked.

'Only in so far as one knows anyone,' said Helen.

'I see,' said the dapper man, because her comment had not really been an answer to his question.

Helen reached out with one long, exquisite finger and stroked the man's lapel. 'I like this fabric,' she said.

'Thanks,' the dapper man said – he was becoming increasingly uncomfortable.

She stared him in the eye and smiled again. She was wearing a black dress with bare shoulders, no jewellery because it felt harsh to her skin, but she had seen many other women wearing it at this gathering and had decided, in her way, that it was a thing she should do. She said, 'If you're turned on, I listen well.'

'Huh?' said the dapper man.

Helen didn't realize that she was making no sense, although she easily picked up on the dapper man's confusion. She was also picking up on the fact that his initial attraction to her was dimming. This was not a good thing. She needed this man. She wanted to take the evening with him. She cast about within the consciousness that passed, in her brain, for intelligence, and soon decided what her next move should be.

She said, 'I'm not available,' and turned away, so her back was to the dapper man.

He stared at her back for a moment – it looked tanned and smooth and exquisite – then tapped her lightly on the shoulder. This act surprised her. At this gathering, she was not prepared for surprises. Her eyes wide, she wheeled about as quickly as the swishing of a cat's tail and raked her fingers across his cheek. Blood flowed at once. His mouth fell open. He touched the scratches on his cheek, and saw the blood on his fingers. He looked confusedly into Helen's eyes, but saw nothing there that he had expected – anger, astonishment, apology, pending explanation. He saw that her eyes were still wide, and that her jaw was set, as if she were going to strike again. He backed a step away from her, mumbled, 'I'm sorry,' although he had no idea what he was sorry for. He backed up another step, saw that Helen's eyes were still on him, that they were still wide, and that her stance was that of an animal waiting to strike – tense, anticipatory. Then, responding to some deep inner voice, he turned and ran from the room.

But Helen had no idea that she had blundered. Even when two dozen pairs of eyes turned accusingly or questioningly or with surprise on her, and even when Martin himself came over and demanded to know what had happened – 'Jesus Christ, do you know who that *is*?' – her thoughts were still on the dapper man himself, and upon the fact that he had aroused in her the same need that had been aroused the previous evening.

She salivated.

A muted growling sound started in her throat.

Smalley had come to Erthmun's apartment to tell him that Internal Affairs would probably call off their investigation, and that Erthmun would be reinstated to active duty within a couple of days.

Erthmun said, 'You woke me up.' He was standing in his blue robe at the open door to his apartment.

'Yes, I can tell,' Smalley said, without a tone of apology. Hell, it wasn't even 9.00 p.m. What was this guy doing asleep?

Erthmun started to close the door; Smalley reached out and stiff-armed it. 'Don't you want to know *why* we're calling off the investigation?'

'Not particularly,' Erthmun answered.

'Shit, that's disappointing,' Smalley said.

'I'm sure it is,' Erthmun said. 'Let go of the fucking door.'

Smalley said, 'We're calling off the investigation because of lack of evidence. Which doesn't mean the evidence doesn't exist.' He quickly added, 'Why do you think this perp stuffs chocolate in the mouths of the victims?'

'Suddenly you're a homicide detective?' Erthmun asked.

'I'm just curious.'

'I don't know why the killer stuffs chocolate into the mouths of his victims,' Erthmun said, and pushed hard on the door, which Smalley was still stiff-arming. 'Back off.'

Smalley let go of the door.

Twenty-four

The following evening, near the house on Four Mile Creek

The woman said to her male companion, 'Do you know what my father used to say about winters up here?'

Her companion looked expectantly at her, but said nothing.

She continued, 'He said they were cold enough to steal the breath from a dead man.' She smiled. 'I always liked that. I'm not sure what it means, but I like it.'

Her companion said, 'I think I know what it means. And it's true.'

The woman took a long, deep breath. Her companion looked on in awe: he knew that if he took such a breath in this frigid air he'd end up doubled over with a fit of coughing. The woman declared, 'It's so bracing, don't you think, Hal?'

'Bracing, sure,' Hal said.

The woman – her name was Denise – grinned at him. 'This isn't your cup of tea, is it?'

'Of course it is,' Hal claimed unconvincingly. 'I'm the first to admit that we can't spend our lives wrapped up tight and warm within the cocoons that we call cities.' He smiled, pleased with his metaphor.

'Agreed,' said Denise. She glanced at her watch; it was closing in on 5.30 p.m. Soon, it would be dark, and the small lean-to where they had planned to spend the night was still a good distance off. She hadn't expected Hal to be so slow. Jesus, he jogged every day.

'Problem?' he said.

Denise glanced at the overcast grey sky. 'Not really. I don't know. It doesn't ... feel right, here.' They were in an open area fringed by evergreens, oaks and tulip trees. The snow was knee deep and heavy, which made it difficult to walk in. '"Doesn't feel right"?' Hal said. 'Could you explain that?' His sudden apprehension was obvious.

She chuckled. 'Only that I think we've got a little weather on the way and that we should pick up the pace if we expect—'

'Weather? You mean a storm?'

She shrugged. 'Possibly. A small storm.' She took her radio from Hal's backpack; it was tuned to a weather channel in Old Forge, fifty miles south. She turned up the volume. Nothing. She cursed, shook the radio, turned it off, then on again. Still nothing. 'Hal, did you put new batteries in this thing?'

He looked sheepishly at her, and started to speak,

but she cut in, 'You didn't, did you?' She could hear the anger in her voice, but decided it was all right – he deserved it.

He said, 'Actually, yes, I did.'

'*New* batteries?'

Another sheepish look. 'Have you checked the price on new batteries, Denise? Jesus, they're a couple of bucks. So, I figured—'

'This isn't a new battery?'

'Sure it is. You know those batteries in the drawer in the kitchen? I used one of them. I even checked it on the battery tester first—'

'Dammit!' Denise whispered.

'I fucked up?' Hal asked.

She put the radio to her ear, turned up the volume all the way, heard nothing, sighed. 'No, Hal, you didn't fuck up. It's all right.'

'But we're in deep shit?'

'Not waist deep. Ankle deep, maybe.' She gave him a quick grin, as if for reassurance. 'Listen, I know this snow is difficult to slog through, and I know you really hate being out here, but do you think that if we put on our snowshoes we could do a couple of miles before it gets too dark?'

'How many is a couple?'

'Three. Maybe four.'

'That's not a couple. That's *several*.'

'Okay, okay. Several miles. Can you do it?'

'Shit, Denise,' he said. 'I jog every day.'

*

His leg cramps began twenty minutes later, when the grey overcast had turned dark grey and a lazy snow-fall had begun. He sat on a tree stump and massaged his thigh. 'This is a very different kind of muscle action I'm employing here than when I jog,' he explained.

They were in a sparse grove of evergreens. Beyond it, to the east, the land sloped severely into pitch darkness; to the west, a few rust-coloured rags of dusk remained. There were no hazy reflections of city lights anywhere on the dark cloud cover, no distant noises of cars or aeroplanes. The air was as still and cold and quiet as stone.

Denise realized all at once that she wasn't absolutely certain of their location. She asked for the compass, which Hal kept in his jacket pocket. He fished it out, gave it to her. She checked it, looked at the dark grey overcast and the lazy snowfall, checked the compass again, gave it back to him, and grinned nervously.

He said, 'Are we knee deep in shit now, Denise?'

Her grin quivered. 'Mid-calf, I'd say.'

'That's very encouraging.'

'Sorry.'

He stood, leaned over, massaged his thigh some more, and said, 'A week from now, we're going to look back on this and say, "Now that was a night to remember."'

She gave him a quick, quivering grin.

He said, 'We *are*, aren't we?'

She said nothing.

'Denise?' he coaxed, and he noticed, then, that her gaze wasn't on him, but subtly beyond him. He turned his head, looked.

She said, 'Hal, I think that's a goddamned house.'

He didn't see it. 'Where?' he said.

'What do you mean "where"? Right there.'

He turned round, so his back was to her, moved forward a few paces, then stepped to his right. The snowfall had picked up; a quirky breeze had started. He thought he was thankful for it, for the whisper it made on the snow and in the trees. He had never been comfortable with silence.

He saw the house, then, though not much of it – a steeply pitched roof, part of the top floor. It was too dark, now, for him to say what kind of windows there were. 'Do you think someone lives in it?' he asked.

'How would I know?' Denise answered. 'It doesn't matter, does it?'

'Goddamned right.'

'I want you to admit one thing to me,' Hal said.

'Oh, yeah? What?' Denise said.

'I want you to admit that you've fucked up. I want to hear you say, "Hal, I've fucked up. It's a first, but I've done it." Can you say that?'

They were standing in deep snow inside the remains of a picket fence. It was very stylized: each picket was flattened at its point, and, just beneath that, much fatter and rounder than normal picket

fences; the body of each picket was very narrow,
except for two points that flared out gracefully
midway down on either side, these points connected
individual pickets with neighbouring pickets. Denise
had said that she liked this design, and Hal had
claimed that he could fashion similar pickets for
their own fence, should they decide at some point
in their relationship to build one. Denise had said,
then, that 'the building of fences is a nest-feathering
occupation'.

They were not far from the house itself, which was
large, grey with age and weather, sturdy-looking, and
clearly empty. Denise said, 'Do you require such a
confession, darling?'

'That you've fucked up. Sure.'

She admitted that she had, and it made him happy.

Then she said, gesturing to indicate the area inside
the fence, 'They liked bushes.'

'Those are forsythia,' Hal declared.

'I know that,' she said.

'Well, then, that makes two of us.'

She looked apologetically at him, then at the house,
which, oddly, looked less forbidding from this vantage
point – inside the friendly picket fence – than it had
when they had first seen it. 'Are we going in?' she
asked.

'Yes,' he said. 'I'm cold.'

Twenty-five

Helen heard the music of living things, which, in this place, was at once dissonant, like the raucous noises of bluejays sparring, and melodic, the wet and powerful noises of sex, which are the noises that scream into the ear of eternity, and she heard the whispers that come from sleep, and the cries and the shouting and the screeches that leaped from the minds of those who dreamed. And she heard the music that was music to other ears, too – Mozart, George Harrison, Marianne Faithfull, John Prine, Samuel Barber – because these were the sounds that living things made to put themselves and their souls and their lives in harmony with the air, the water, and the earth.

Helen's life was music, which was sex, which was food, which was music, and sex, and food, which was one thing, which was Helen.

The dapper man, wrapped only in a towel, and

peeking around the open door to his apartment, said, 'My God, how did you get in here?' because the building was secure, of course. Smells were wafting out from within the apartment, a mixture of beef, mushrooms, cheese, and red wine, and they got Helen's saliva flowing again. And there was Hank Williams on the CD player, because the dapper man loved Hank Williams, although he played him only when he was alone. How she got into the building was of little concern to Helen. She did what she needed to do. She had needed to get into the building; she got in. She said now, 'I need you.'

'You *need* me?' The dapper man was astonished, confused. Without knowing he was doing it, he touched the fresh bandages on his cheek, and repeated, 'You *need* me?' and added, 'For what?'

Helen did not recognize such questions. She barely recognized questions as questions. They indicated uncertainty, which was not a part of her existence. She said, 'You!' and swept past him, and shredded his stomach with her graceful fingers as she did so, and when she was inside, and had turned to face him, he had begun to double over from the pain she had inflicted, and his gaze was rising questioningly to meet hers, to find some answer in her sky-blue eyes. *Why do you want to hurt me?* his gaze said.

But there were no answers in her eyes, and no questions in them, either. There was need, and hunger, and certainty.

*

'It's very dark,' Hal said.

'That's because there aren't any lights,' Denise said.

'Do you think this is safe?'

'What do you mean? The floor? Are you asking if the floor is safe? It feels safe.' She lifted one foot and brought it down softly; it made a slight whumping noise. 'See, safe enough.' She thought that she was babbling, trying to find solace in the sound of her own voice. But solace from what?

Hal said, 'There should be lights.'

'And room service, too,' Denise said.

'Okay, so what do we do now? Spread our sleeping bags out here?'

'No.' She bent over and held her hand near the bottom of the front door; 'See,' she said. 'Feel that draught? Jesus, we'll be popsicles by morning.'

'I thought our sleeping bags were rated at twenty below.'

'I really think that our best bet is to find some inner room and sleep there,' Denise said.

'Inner room where? Down here? Upstairs?'

'I don't think it matters.'

'Maybe there's a fireplace. I mean, there *has* to be a fireplace.'

'I'm sure there's a fireplace.' She looked at him: his face was only an elongated oval a little paler than the darkness in the house. 'But I'm just as sure we shouldn't use it. I'd say that birds have been building nests in the chimney for a couple of decades. We might light a fire and fill the whole damned place with smoke.'

'Oh, sure,' Hal said, sounding chastened. 'You're right. That was stupid.'

She looked at him, again. Her eyes were beginning to adjust to the low light. She could see his features swimming on the creamy oval that was his face. 'Am I a bitch?' she said.

And he answered, too quickly, she thought, 'No. You're not a bitch.'

She sighed. 'I treat you badly sometimes, don't I?'

'No more than I deserve,' he said. 'Why are you suddenly assuming your "true confessions" mode?'

This surprised her. 'What's that? I'm just trying to be honest – fair.'

'I understand that's what you're doing. But why here, and now?'

It was a good question, she thought. 'Because I'm a . . . fair and honest person,' she said.

'Oh.'

A tall window, covered by the sad remains of a lace curtain, stood near the front door. Remarkably, all the glass was intact, and, judging from the motionless air in the house, all the window glass on the entire first floor was probably intact as well. Denise stepped over to the window, peered out, and said, 'You know what, it doesn't look too bad out there, Hal.'

'Meaning?'

She straightened. 'I think the snow has stopped.'

'You're not suggesting we go and look for the damned lean-to in the dark, are you?'

She shook her head briskly. 'Of course not. I was simply making an observation. It's not snowing any more.'

A brief and incoherent whisper crept out of the darkness in the house and made them fall silent for a moment.

Denise said, 'What was that, do you think?'

Hal said, 'I don't know. Nothing important.'

She glanced at him. 'Nothing important?' She smiled. 'What would have made it important?'

'I don't know,' he said again.

'I don't, either,' Denise said.

Another whisper crept out of the darkness in the house. But it was not incoherent. It was almost a sentence: 'The damned lean-to in the dark.'

Hal said, 'It's a damned echo.'

Denise said. 'It would have to be a very weird echo, Hal.'

They heard birdsong then. It was extended, tremulous, beautiful; it filled the dark house. And when it was done, Hal said, 'A bird.'

'Yes, a bird,' Denise whispered, as if in awe.

'Yes,' they heard from within the bowels of the house, 'a bird.'

'Nothing important,' said the voice of the house.

They fell silent. The house fell silent. After several minutes, Hal said, 'These phenomena must be repeatable.'

Denise looked at him and forced a grin. 'Huh?'

He said again, with emphasis now, 'These phenomena must be repeatable. It's a respected tenet of science. In the face of unexplainable events, those events must demonstrate repeatability. Take the Search for Extraterrestrial Intelligence, for instance. Do you know what that is?'

'Of course I do.'

'Okay. In the past thirty years of that endeavour, there have been numerous instances of strange, apparently directed radio transmissions from sources beyond our solar system. But none of these radio transmissions has ever demonstrated repeatability, and so scientists have concluded that they are simply random events of little or no significance.' He had more to say, but he realized that he was babbling. He finished, 'I'm babbling.'

'It's all right,' she said.

'And there's something else, too. I've got to pee.'

'Thank you for sharing.'

'And I think what I'm going to do – ' he reached behind him and pulled a flashlight from his backpack; it was something he should have done before they stepped into the house, he realized ' – is find the downstairs bathroom.'

'You're kidding.'

'Kidding?' He turned the flashlight on and shone it in Denise's eyes. She squinted because of the light and told him he was being an asshole, but he was happy to see her face. 'Why would I be kidding?' he said, and shone the flashlight briefly up the stairs in front of them, and to the left, into a huge, open room. There was no furniture in it, but there was a thick layer of dust on the floor, and the footprints of bare feet in the dust.

'Look there,' he said.

'Yes, I see,' Denise said. 'Kids come in here and play. It's fun. I used to do it myself when I was a kid – go into an old house and play.'

'Kids from where, for God's sake?' he said. 'We're twenty miles from any kids.'

Denise thought about this; he was right of course, she realized. And why would *these* children be bare-foot in winter? 'I don't know,' she said.

The footprints in the dust were fresh because the hardwood floor was visible beneath them. Denise pointed this out, and Hal told her she didn't need to point it out, but then he said, 'They're small foot-prints. They're just kid's footprints, like you said.'

And another whisper wafted out of the bowels of the house. It was followed by birdsong, and by the chortling of toads, and the twittering of crickets, as if they were walking in a meadow in summer.

Denise, her own voice at a whisper, said, 'What the hell *is* that?'

'Only what it sounds like,' Hal said.

'Jesus, I don't *know* what it sounds like,' Denise said. After a moment, she added, 'We should leave, Hal. I get an awful feeling here.'

But there were no whispers in the house, then, and

no chortling of toads, no echoes. A creeper of wind had snuck in from somewhere and obliterated the footprints in the dust. Hal pointed out that they weren't that fresh, after all, look at them. And Denise said that maybe he was right. What choice did they have, really? The night had thrust them unawares into a life and death situation, and they had to make the most of it.

'Yes,' Hal agreed glumly. 'We do.'

Denise cupped her hands around her mouth. 'Hello,' she shouted.

'Hello,' they heard from within the house.

'Hello,' she called again. 'Is anyone there?'

'Is anyone there?' the voices of the house replied.

Then Hal said, 'I don't think we're alone here,' and shone his flashlight about frantically. Its yellow beam caught what looked like insects speeding through the cold air.

'Insects,' Denise said.

Hal let the light settle. Its beam was on a far wall – white plaster, orange wainscoting. A naked form – stomach, pubic hair, teeth, breasts, sky-blue eyes – stepped quickly and gracefully into the light, then was gone.

'Jesus Christ,' Denise whispered.

Another naked form appeared in the light, and was gone. Then another, gone. And another. Gone. And then they were like insects moving through the light, and Denise whispered, 'I'm sorry. God, I'm sorry.'

Because these, they knew, were the *others* in the

house. They were on the stairs in front of them, and in the big room where the footprints had been. They were close enough to touch, and no more visible than shadows on a starlit night. But they were real, and they moved with purpose, and grace, and terrible certainty.

Twenty-six

Erthmun thought that he should be asleep, but he couldn't sleep because he had a joke to tell. It was a joke of his own devising and he thought it was very funny. It was his first joke, the only joke he had ever devised, and he was desperate to share it, but there was no one available to share it with. He had tried calling Patricia David, but had only got her machine. He'd tried calling the squad room, but no one was there tonight whom he saw regularly on the day shift, and he felt self-conscious at the idea of telling his first joke to a stranger. He'd even tried calling his sister, Lila, but she wasn't at home either.

So he sat on the edge of his bed and he said to himself, 'I have a wonderful joke but no one to share it with.' It was pathetic, he thought. *He* was pathetic. For God's sake, *everyone* should have someone they could tell a joke to at a moment's notice.

And, for the second time in a week, he felt very lonely, and very alone.

The woman in the hall, he thought. The woman with the big cat in the hall. Maybe she'd like to hear his joke. She had a kind of bond with him, after all. They had had an encounter in the hall. She had stolen a glance at his erection beneath his blue robe, and he had fantasized bending her over the bed. Surely that was a bond of sorts.

He went to his door, opened it, went out into the hallway, stopped. Where did she live? he wondered. Which apartment? He looked left, right. Hadn't her big grey cat been at the end of the hallway to his left? Sure. Left.

But maybe right.

He looked to his right, tried to visualize the cat at the end of the hallway, there. But he could visualize nothing. He looked to his left again, tried to visualize the cat there. Still nothing.

Shit.

He decided that he'd knock on doors. She lived on the same damned floor – he knew that much about her, anyway.

He looked down at himself, thinking he might be naked. He saw that he wasn't. He was wearing blue jeans, a white shirt, red socks. He grinned. Why would he have to look at himself to find out if he was naked? That was foolish.

He went to a door in the hallway to his left and

knocked. The door was number 4C, and no one answered his knock. He knocked again, said, 'Hello?' but still no one answered his knock. He decided that no one was home, went to apartment 4D, and knocked there.

Almost at once a tall thin man sporting a trendy handlebar moustache answered Erthmun's knock. He looked annoyed and Erthmun guessed that he was upset at being interrupted while doing something personal.

'I'm sorry,' Erthmun said, 'wrong apartment,' because he was not about to tell his joke to someone who was clearly angry with him, and someone who was, besides, a complete stranger.

The man silently closed his door.

Erthmun went to apartment 4E and knocked. Within moments the woman he had seen a week earlier answered his knock. She was carrying her big grey cat in her arms and she was dressed in the same blue robe Erthmun had first seen her in. She smiled ingratiatingly and said, 'Mr Erthmun, how pleasant to see you.' She was stroking her cat, and as she said these words, her stroking action quickened, as if, Erthmun guessed, his appearance at her door actually *had* given her pleasure.

He gave her his most ingratiating smile in return and asked, 'Do you have time for a joke?'

'A joke?' She looked suddenly perplexed.

He nodded vigorously; her expression became one

of concern. 'Yes,' he explained hurriedly. 'I made up a joke ...' He smiled ingratiatingly again. 'What's your name? I think I should know your name.'

'My name?' She had stopped stroking her cat.

Erthmun said, 'My name's Jack.'

She said, 'Cindy,' and put her hand on the open door, as if getting ready to close it.

He nodded, as if accepting the fact of her name, and hurried on, 'May I come in to tell you my joke, Cindy?'

She shook her head. 'No, I don't think so.'

It took a moment for her rejection to sink in. He backed away from the door, felt suddenly very embarrassed, said, 'Sorry. My mistake,' and went back quickly to his apartment.

He sat on the edge of his bed.

He called Patricia David's number again, but without success. He tried Lila's number again, too, but without success. He tried his mother's number: it was busy.

He got off his bed, went to his window, put his hands flat on the window sill, locked his arms, and said, into the myriad lights of Manhattan, 'There was a man who was waiting for his wife to have quadruplets. The man knew that his wife was going to have quadruplets because the doctor had performed an ultra-sound exam. While he waited for his wife to have quadruplets, the man tried to devise some names. Maxwell, Hiram, George, Terry, Bud. But he liked none of these names, and he thought that he had better wait until the quadruplets were born before trying to devise names. Then he was called into the delivery room, where he watched as his wife gave birth first to one son, then another, then another, and still another. He smiled and said to the doctors present, and pointing at the babies, "That's Ted, that's Fred, that's Ed, and that's Ned." Then he thought about this, realized what he had done and said, "My, how rhyme flies when you're having sons."' Erthmun smiled. It was a good joke. *My, how rhyme flies when you're having sons*. A pun. A play on words. His first joke had been a play on words. Didn't that say volumes about him and about his ... humanity? Didn't that prove *something*?

The woman was blue-eyed and auburn-haired, and she had been told more than once that this was a stunning combination. She had also been asked more than once where it came from. Some topsy-turvy intermingling of genes, a Swedish father and a Mediterranean mother? She had grown tired of such questions, and, now, when they were asked, she became surly and uncommunicative. She didn't know why. She was not normally like that. She was normally vivacious and outgoing. In the past month, she had even bought green contact lenses to ward off the questions, but they felt harsh on her eyes, so she did not often wear them.

Her name was Greta, and she was twenty-seven years old. She was a copywriter for an advertising firm on 42nd Street, and she lived near Central Park in a studio apartment whose only window looked out on the Park. Greta had spent many nights and days staring out of that window at the Park, because the view called up her formative years on her parents' farm in northern Pennsylvania, when her second storey window looked out on a similar landscape.

On several of the nights that she had looked out at the Park she had seen Helen. It did not occur to her that she was seeing anything unusual; she supposed that she was seeing some odd movement of air and leaves and snow, something that only for the briefest moment became a naked human form and then instantly coalesced into air again, roadway, tree trunk, streetlamp, dust, heat; and so, Greta supposed, she was seeing nothing, not even a brief fantasy.

This night, she saw no dust, and there was no heat. Snow covered the park, except for the roadways which were used often during the day, and they were dark and narrow. The snow tangled in tree limbs, dipped like a garland over the tops of bridges, held fast and fat to the tops of benches.

Greta could see all of this and much more from her studio apartment. She paid well for the view; she had even given up one meal a day for it, and this was a great sacrifice because eating, and eating well, was one of the great pleasures of her life.

She thought that she liked her view of the Park most at night because she could easily work her childhood landscape into it. There were no blue-suited joggers at night, and few yellow cabs, few people sledding or skiing. Occasionally, a horse-drawn hansom cab crossed her field of view, and she especially enjoyed this because she had owned a horse on the farm in Pennsylvania.

It had never occurred to her to go into the Park at night. She thought of herself as a sensible woman and she knew that, even in winter, the Park was not a safe place, especially at night.

But she supposed that, this night, it would be all right simply to go to the edges of the Park and peer in. What could be wrong with that? There were people walking on Central Park West. She would be one of them, and she would peer into the Park, and what she would see there, up close, would feed the nostalgic fantasy she had indulged in so often at her window.

She thought that she would have to be impulsive about this because if she wasn't impulsive, then she would decide not to do it, and so would probably *never* do it. She thought that she had to cultivate her impulsiveness, that the city was squashing it, some-how, that, as a child, her every act had seemed impulsive and capricious and whimsical. She did not come here to have the child within her squashed by this big and impersonal place.

She got into her green leather coat, which covered her to mid-calf, put on her brown leather gloves, and her slip-on boots, studied herself in the full-length mirror near the door, decided she looked good, but needed her hat, got it out of the closet, put it on – it was a red beret and very stylish – and left her apartment.

She was on the street within a minute and trying to decide whether to cross at the light, a block away, or wait for traffic to clear and then jaywalk. She'd been ticketed for jaywalking, and it had been an unpleasant experience in a city that had made her no stranger to unpleasant experiences.

Shit, she thought, who was going to see her jaywalk here, at night? She waited for the traffic to clear, crossed Central Park West to the sidewalk, hesitated a few feet from a tall wrought-iron fence, then crossed to the fence itself, put her hands on the bars, and felt the cold of the black iron through her leather gloves.

She put her face between the bars and peered into the Park.

She saw little. There were tall, snow-covered bushes in front of her, and she could see a triangle of snow-covered grass between them. She let go of the fence, stepped back. This was all very disappointing. She'd have to find some other place to look into the Park.

She went back to the sidewalk, saw a young couple walking towards her, felt suddenly foolish and self-conscious, and began walking quickly away from them. Why was she doing this? she asked herself as she walked. She had no answer. She was acting under an impulse that was unknown to her. This made her happy.

She walked faster.

After a minute, she looked behind her and saw that the young couple was gone and that the sidewalk was empty. Five blocks south, she could see traffic moving slowly on Columbus Circle. She found it astonishing that she had walked so far in so short a time.

She looked towards the Park. There was no wrought-iron fence here, only a waist-high stone wall. She thought she could easily climb it, which was an idea that appealed to her because it involved another impulsive act whose origin was shrouded somewhere in the mystery that was her sub-conscious.

But she did not move at once. She ruminated upon the idea for several moments. She tossed the pros and cons about in her head. She asked herself, *What if there is someone just beyond that stone wall, and he's waiting for a fool like me to venture into the Park?* And she answered herself, *What fool, indeed, would be waiting there at night, in the frigid cold?* It was a good question, she thought.

At last, she crossed the little strip of snow-covered grass to the wall, hesitated only a moment, put a foot up on the wall, and climbed over it, into the Park.

She smiled. This, she thought, was much better, though the deep snow here was cold on her bare calves, and was already beginning to make its way down her boots.

She saw much. Paths winding like a tangled Mobius strip through the Park, snow tumbling through the dark sky, birds shivering in their pitiful spaces, the wretched homeless making the most of their cardboard shelters in the Park's secluded areas, ice on the lake cracking under the weight of cold and atmosphere.

She thought she had never seen so much with such startling clarity.

She thought she had stumbled upon some great hidden talent.

She heard movement nearby.

Her breathing stopped.

Who's there? her brain demanded.

A shadow appeared not far away. It was a little darker than the snow, and it was tall. It moved towards her with deliberation. In a man's voice, it said, 'You're a damned fool!'

Go away! her brain screamed.

'A damned fool!'

'I have mace!' her mouth screamed.

'Use it, then!'

She took a quick glance behind her, at the stone wall. It was right there, at her heels; she needed only sit on it, tumble backwards, do a little reverse somersault back into the city's spaces, out of this awful place.

'Use it!' the man demanded again.

But she did not do a reverse somersault.

And the man came quickly at her.

Twenty-seven

'You look pretty much like shit, Jack,' Patricia David
said. Erthmun was seated at his desk, opposite hers;
it was his first day of reinstatement.

'Uh-huh,' Erthmun said. 'I wish I felt as good as I
looked.'

'Maybe you should go home. What is it – the flu?'

'The flu? Who knows?'

She told him that the mayor's nephew had been
murdered two nights previously and that they might
be assigned the case. He said, 'The mayor's nephew?'
and Patricia gave him the man's name.

'I am not one of the mayor's fans,' Erthmun said,
and Patricia told him that the remark was a non
sequitur.

'What does it matter if you're one of the mayor's
fans or not?' she asked.

He said confusedly that he didn't know what difference it made, then asked, 'Do you want to hear a joke, Patricia?'

She smiled at him across her desk. 'A joke? This is a first.'

'It's not a good joke. It's a crummy joke. But it's mine.'

Patricia was a little surprised at how earnest he seemed, and at how urgently he needed to tell his joke. She said, 'Sure. Tell me your joke.'

He told it to her. He delivered it haltingly, as if he were devising it all over again, and when he was done, Patricia looked blankly at him and said, 'I don't get it.'

He sighed. 'I told you it was a bad joke. Let's go to work.'

'No, no. Please. Explain it – "how rhyme flies when you're having sons". I think that I *should* get it, Jack, but I don't, and it makes me feel stupid. I don't like to feel stupid the first thing in the morning.'

'You're putting me on, right?' Erthmun said.

She smiled.

'Right?' he said again.

'Yes,' she admitted. 'I am. I mean, one bad joke deserves another, right?' She passed an eight-by-ten-inch photograph across the desk to him. 'This is the mayor's late nephew,' she said. 'As you can see, Jack, he's been cannibalized. It's not in all the papers, but it appears to be working into something of a trend.'

*

Dog-walking was a pleasant early-morning occupation, the old man thought. If the dog was well trained – as his was – then it was not strenuous exercise, but it was exercise. It wasn't dangerous, either, because people stayed away from big dogs on stout leashes, and so he – the old man – could content himself with whatever daydream was current.

He was walking in Central Park, on a path that wasn't often used because it wound into a thick stand of trees. He had used this route often, however, and no one had ever bothered him because of his dog, whose name was Friday. The dog was as gentle as a baby's laugh, but it looked fierce and wolf-like.

The old man's head moved a lot as he walked, not because of a nervous condition, but because he liked to see what was going on around him. Usually, on these walks, there was little to see that he had not seen a thousand times before, but he looked anyway because he liked catching a glimpse of the occasional squirrel or chipmunk or cardinal, and because he was interested in more than simply the narrow dirt path and his dog's rear end beneath its upturned white tail.

The bright morning sunlight reflected off the new snow and into the old man's eyes, which made him squint. When he walked into shadow out of the bright sunlight and no longer needed to squint, the world around him darkened, then brightened slowly, and images shimmered.

He thought at first, seeing this way, that the man sitting up against a tree not far off the path was wearing a rust-coloured jogger's uniform, but then his eyes adjusted and he saw that the man was naked, and that he was covered with blood. He saw also that the man's mouth was wide open and that something dark had been stuffed into it. The old man could smell the stuff – he was not far off.

He stopped walking, whispered a curse, and realized what he was looking at. Friday tugged hard at the leash in his frantic efforts to get at the man sitting against the tree. The smells were so delightful to his canine nose – blood, chocolate.

'Dammit, dog!' the old man shouted. But it was no use. Friday was simply too strong for him.

She was blue-eyed and auburn-haired, her name was Greta, and she had been having strange and confusing lapses of memory in the past couple of months. She remembered leaving her apartment the previous evening on some odd mission to discover Central Park at night, but remembered nothing concrete beyond shutting her door behind her.

And now there was a rust-coloured residue in her bathtub, her beautiful green leather coat was missing and her boots were smeared with blood. And as she peered out of her studio apartment window at Central Park five storeys below, she could see flashing lights. She knew that they were cop cars. She knew, also,

that they were there, in the Park, because of something *she* had done.

She was fascinated.

A memory came to her all at once. It was a memory
from her childhood, and it bore a wonderful mixture
of pleasure and pain. She saw the face of a young boy
in it. He had dark eyes and tousled red hair, and she
thought that she had heard him running towards her
through tall grasses. Then he was simply ... *there*,
looking down at her. She thought that, in her
memory, she could hear a stream moving close by.
And she could smell the tangy odour of the earth,
and could see the face of a doll lying in her lap. It was
a strange face. It had no eyes, only crumpled pieces
of brightly coloured paper where the eyes should
have been, and mud had been stuffed in the mouth.

'Why'd you do that?' she remembered the boy
asking.

Then the memory was gone, and try as she might –
because it gave her so much delicious pleasure and
pain – she could not get it back.

Patricia David, driving, exclaimed, 'Jack, you look
positively *green*,' and then gave him a worried grin
that was designed to tell him that he didn't actually
look green, but that he did look very sick.

He leaned forward a little, adjusted the rear-view
mirror so he could see his reflection and sat back
without saying anything.

Patricia said, 'I think I should take you home.'

'Home,' he said, and it sounded to Patricia like a question, though she guessed that it wasn't.

She said, 'I think you should rest, Jack.' She stopped at a red light. 'Shit, why don't I turn here and go back down Lexington, and I'll take you home?'

'Home?' Erthmun said, and this time Patricia recognized that it *was* a question.

'Home, yes,' she said. 'To your little apartment.'

'Apartment,' he said.

The light changed; Patricia made a left on her way to Lexington, made a quick stop for a lanky, hollow-faced jay-walking man in an army coat and blue knitted cap, swore beneath her breath, then got going again when the man had crossed. She said, 'Apartment, yes. Home. The place you live. The place you hang your hat. The place where you eat and do all your personal little things.'

'No,' he said.

'No? No what?' She grinned at him again. He was huddled against the door, legs up, knees together, arms across his chest. His eyes were all but closed, and his mouth was shut tightly. He looked cold. She said, 'Are you cold, Jack?'

'Yes,' he whispered.

'Do you want me to turn the heater up?'

'Heater up? Yes.'

'Jack, Christ,' she turned up the heater, 'I'm worried about you. Maybe instead of taking you home I should take you to the hospital.'

'Hospital. No,' he whispered.

She pulled over so she was double-parked in front of a deli called Sam's. She put the car in 'park', leaned over the seat, laid the back of her hand gently against Erthmun's forehead, and held it there a moment, surprised that he was making no protest. She withdrew her hand. 'You don't seem to have a fever, Jack.'

'No,' he managed. 'I'm just damned cold.'

'I turned the heat up.'

He said nothing.

'Do you want me to turn it up more?'

'Turn it up more? No. Thanks. Just take me . . . to my apartment.'

'Right away,' she said.

Twenty-eight

Thirty-four years earlier, in the house on Four Mile Creek

Thomas Erthmun maintained that fear from his children was more important than love because love was a fuzzy, undependable emotion. He was saying, 'Jack, if you don't obey your mother, then it will be a very hard night for you when I return, do you understand?'

Jack's three-year-old eyes looked up at the man and Jack thought, not for the first time, that the man was bigger than trees, or mountains, and scarier than anything, and he wasn't easy to fool, either, because he seemed to know everything that Jack thought as if he had thought it, too. Jack nodded, wide-eyed, open-mouthed, and said, 'Yes, Daddy.'

The man said, 'Of course you do, son,' and then leaned over and briefly kissed his wife, who was

holding Jack, which provided the boy with a whiff of
the man's aftershave, and of the man's recently eaten
breakfast – oatmeal, a generous slice of ham, a glass
of orange juice and a cup of coffee – and then Jack
felt the man lay a hand gently on his cheek. He
winced in anticipation.

Jack's mother said, 'Have a safe journey, Thomas.'

'I will,' the man said.

And then he lifted his hand and pinched Jack's
cheek hard enough to hurt. Then he said smilingly,
'And if you do not obey your mother, son, then that
will be the least of your pain, do you understand?'

'Understand?' Jack echoed. 'Yes, Daddy.' He knew
enough not to touch his throbbing cheek. He felt his
mother back a step away from the man, who turned
quickly, and was out of the door a moment later.

Jack looked at his mother. He read several emotions
in her, some of which he felt himself – fear, gratitude
that the man was gone, but loneliness, too, which
Jack had yet to feel. There was another emotion in
her that Jack didn't understand; he sensed only that
it made the woman look at herself as if in a mirror
and see someone there whom she barely recognized.

He sensed, also, that she was going to set him down
and tell him to go outside and play. He did not want
this. He loved being close to her, loved being held by
her, loved following her about the house as she
tended to chores, loved her voice, even when she was
scolding him, loved her eyes on him, loved her smell
and her whispers and her smiles.

And then she set him down, despite his protests, leaned over, kissed him gently on the same cheek that his father had pinched, and told him he could go and play.

Jack looked pleadingly up at her.

'Go ahead,' she coaxed.

'I don't want to,' Jack said.

'It's a beautiful day, Jackie. The sun is warm. Go outside and play.' An edge of impatience had crept into her voice, and he knew that if he didn't do as she'd asked, the air around her would grow dark and he would hardly recognize her as his mother.

'Okay,' he said, and there was the hint of defiance in his voice. He went to the front door, glanced back, saw that she was smiling, but knew it was the kind of smile that accompanied her need to be free of him. So he went out to the yard, where his sisters were playing hide and seek among the hydrangeas.

He saw his eldest sister, Sylvia, first. She had taken up a position behind a very tall hydrangea near the picket fence that Uncle Jack had built. When she saw her brother, she put her finger to her lips to tell him not to give away her position to Lila, who was nowhere in sight.

He only looked at her.

She made pushing motions with her hand to tell him to go away.

This was all right; he had no need to play with his sisters – he preferred playing alone. But, at that moment, he most wanted to be with his mother, in the house. He wanted her to kiss his cheek again, where his father had pinched it, and he wanted to follow her around and smell her sweet smell and watch her do all the things that she did during the day. But he knew that she didn't want him in the house with her, and it was something he understood, in a primitive way, and accepted. But he didn't know what else to do.

Sylvia made pushing motions at him again, and added, in a whisper, 'Go away, Jackie.'

Lila appeared then. She was younger than Sylvia by a year and a half, but she was taller, and prettier, and Jack liked her better because she often listened to him when she thought that he had something to say.

He looked blankly again at Sylvia, and then wandered from the yard, past the ornate picket fence, and into the tall fields beyond.

This morning these fields were alive with honey-bees and warm sunlight. They smelled of wet earth, which was a smell that excited Jack and gave him an odd, pleasurable feeling that he hoped his father didn't know about – he seemed to know about so many things.

Then, quickly enough, he was beyond the noises of his sisters at play, beyond the smells of the house itself – which, for Jack, lingered for days, weeks. They were the smells of baking, cleaning, and the commingled odours of his father's sweat and his mother's perfume.

Then the house itself was beyond his view, and he

knew all at once that he had gone far from his mother and his home.

He ran.

No one in his family had ever seen him run. If they had, they would have been astonished. They would have said, 'How can such a little fireplug run like that?' He had told Lila how much he liked to run, and he'd asked her to come out in the fields and run with him, but she told him that, although she'd like to, it was not a thing that young girls did, and he had read regret in her.

He ran this morning for hours. The tall grasses passed him by as a whir of green and brown. Insects tried to hop out of his way, but he trampled many underfoot and others hopped headlong into him.

He smiled as he ran. He laughed, too. And as he ran, he could hear the laughter of others. It came to him briefly that he was hearing only an echo from somewhere in the high hills that surrounded these fields, although some of the laughter – if he had stopped to listen – clearly came not only from the high hills, but from the trees, too, and from the tall grasses.

Then, at noon, he was finished running and out of breath, at last, so he made his way back to his house and sat at the dining room table – which was one of his favourite places to be – and ate a hearty lunch of meat and fruit.

Twenty-nine

Helen saw the snow and knew that it was temporary.

Months earlier, she had seen birds flying south and she had known that their leavetaking was temporary.

She had watched daylight come, and had known that it was temporary.

She'd seen clouds covering the sun, people walking stiffly against wind and cold, ice forming on the lake in the Park, butterflies emerging from their cocoons in summer, and she had known that it was all temporary.

Just as she knew that *she* was temporary.

She could not have given voice to this fact, even if she had wanted to – it was real, *she* was real, and now the time was coming when she would not be real. It was all right, because the earth – which was her mother and her father – was not temporary. The earth was eternal, so *she* was eternal. And she was temporary.

She could feel her own disintegration starting. It was like a flower that had begun to blossom slowly deep within her.

And it exhilarated her.

The two young people were new to homelessness. They had assumed, not too long ago, that they were immune to it, that their jobs and their place in society were secure, that such awful things as homelessness happened only to other people. They had even had long discussions about the kind of society that would accept such things as homelessness. The man had postulated that if a label, 'The homeless', is assigned to a group of people, it gave them a kind of awful validity which meant that others in society could pity them but didn't really have to help them. Their label was 'the homeless', just as others were 'the sick', or 'the rich', or 'the working poor'.

But then one unfortunate and unforeseen event piled on top of another, and, in a few months, the young couple found themselves penniless and on the street. They had no family to turn to, no place to go, and no prospects for improvement, except in the eyes of the New York County Welfare Department, which deemed them 'employable' and denied them benefits.

It was a great comfort to them that they had each other. They also thought, at first, that it was probably fortunate that this thing had happened to them in a city like New York, where there were a number of places they could find shelter from the winter nights.

There were Salvation Army missions, places underground – they had heard many stories about what lay beneath Grand Central station: *Beauty and the Beast* had been one of their favourite TV shows – and countless abandoned buildings within a few minutes' walk. Certainly, with all that to choose from, they could find a safe place to spend their nights.

He was tall and lanky, and he had quickly begun to look unhealthy – 'Gaunt,' his wife told him – after they had found themselves on the street. He wore a blue knitted cap that had been given to him by a beloved aunt, now dead, and an army coat that offered him more protection from the cold than any other coat he had owned. He had caught glimpses of himself in shop windows and had thought each time that he really did look like the archetypal homeless man, which made him terribly sad.

This day, he and his wife had decided to leave Manhattan. They thought they could walk across the George Washington Bridge and make their way downstate, through Delaware, eventually, and then into Maryland and finally back to South Carolina, which was where both had been born. They had no real plan about what they were going to eat, or where they were going to sleep. They knew only that the city had worked its grim magic on them, that there really was no safe place to spend their nights, and that if they wanted to put their lives back on track, the first big step was to leave Manhattan, which, they told themselves, they had never liked much anyway. It was a desperate idea, but it was their only idea.

Erthmun sat huddled in his coat and two blankets at his white enamel table, near his open window. He had turned the heat up to maximum, and he could hear the radiators clicking as hot water raced into them.

A cold breeze was blowing on him from the open window, but it touched just his face, the only part of his body that was exposed. The idea that he should close the window was never far from his mind, and he wasn't sure, either, why he had opened it in the first place. He realized that, in the past few weeks, he had become an enigma, not only to Patricia David, Mark Smalley and the woman down the hall, but to himself. It was painful not to know the reasons for the things he did. It made his future, his present and even his past seem uncertain and treacherous.

He wished that he had kept a photo album. It would have thousands of photographs in it and they would show not only him but all the people in his life, from the moment of his birth. They would show his sisters, his mother and his dead father. They would show all the women he had slept with, and all the murder victims whose eyes or wounds or lives he had looked into – the woman in Central Park who'd had her throat slashed and her red wig stolen, the woman in Harlem whose husband had shot her first with a handgun, then with a shotgun and, finally, had put an arrow through her heart, all in an effort, he said, 'to destroy the evil that settled in her' when she joined a weight-loss club. The man on 42nd Street who had simply been beaten to death for his wallet. The family on Long Island who had been variously shot, drowned and stabbed, and then incinerated by a perpetrator who had never been caught. And a thousand other victims, some unique, most mundane, culminating in the women who had had cheap chocolate stuffed in their mouths and their faces cleansed.

And all the photographs in his personal photo album would be in black and white because that was the way he saw scenes from his past – in black and white.

Except for his birth.

Which was a world of colour, and pleasure and pain.

His phone rang.

He let it ring until it stopped.

'Dammit!' Patricia David whispered. Where the hell was he? She'd dropped him at his apartment only an hour and a half earlier, and he had seemed to want only to go to bed and get warm. She tried his number again, let it ring nearly two dozen times, hung up. She wished he had a goddamned answering machine, like everyone else.

She decided that she'd have to go back to his apartment. He was probably asleep, and it wasn't hard to imagine that in his condition he could sleep through a ringing telephone.

She looked at McBride, who was standing at a file cabinet nearby and was obviously waiting for her to acknowledge him. 'I'm going to Erthmun's apartment,' she said.

'You can't,' McBride told her. 'The lieutenant says he needs us both on this, like now!'

'It's too bad,' Patricia said, standing and shrugging into her coat.

'Is that what I tell the lieutenant?'

'Sure. Tell him it's too bad. Use those words exactly.' And she walked briskly past him and out of the squad room.

Erthmun saw his face in his memory. It was in shades of black and white, too. Round and jowly, dark-eyed, thick-lipped, heavy-lidded and prematurely aged. He hoped that it wasn't the face that other people saw. He hoped it was a kind of quirky Dorian Gray portrait that only he could see.

It occurred to him all at once that he had done a lot of sitting at this window, had watched a lot of people passing by. Thousands, maybe. Thousands of victims and thousands of passers-by.

He became aware that something strange was happening inside him. As if some anonymous thing deep within his biology were bursting or blossoming slowly. This frightened him. He thought it foretold his death, and he did not want to die. He thought again about his uncle Jack and his last words – 'Oh, shit!' – which demonstrated such lazy and damnable resignation in the face of death. He – Jack Erthmun – wasn't going to die that way. He would fight Death, he would spit it in the eye and blind it so it wouldn't recognize him. No one was going to shovel him into a rectangle of earth without a lot of kicking and screaming!

So what, he wondered, was he doing at this open window, wrapped up in his cocoon of blankets, waiting for that anonymous thing inside him to burst? It was almost as if he were *offering* himself to it.

In his mind's eye, he saw himself throwing off the blankets, slamming the window shut, fighting the onslaught of death, if only with *action* and *movement* and *noise*.

But it was a fantasy. He did not move from his cocoon of blankets, the cold breeze pushed hard against his face, and he felt the thing inside him blossoming, opening, as if it were about to consume his internal organs slowly from the inside and leave him nothing but a shell of skin and hair, jowls and heavy eyelids.

And suddenly he found that this was a gratifying and pleasant thing. It spoke of some great inevitability that he had long denied and, with that denial, pushed back – as if he had lived his entire life tottering on one leg, afraid to fall. What right did he have to scream into the face of eternity?

*

Helen didn't know how long she had, and it didn't matter. A week. A month. An hour. She would be what she was until she came apart, and then the flies and the burying beetles could have her. She had made food of the living. Soon she would be food *for* the living, and that irony wasn't something she easily understood. She was breasts, pubic hair, gut, teeth, palate, heart, legs and hunger.

She was hungry, now.

And so she would eat.

Thirty

The young homeless couple was peering in a shop window at TV sets. They were both thinking that it would be nice if they had even one room to live in and that room had a TV set in it. They wouldn't even need a remote control. The TV set could have an old-fashioned rotary dial; they wouldn't mind at all getting up from the bed or their chairs to change channels. And it didn't need to be a colour set, either, and it didn't need to be hooked up to cable. Three channels would be fine. *Two* channels would be fine.

They were on 161st Street and they had been on their way out of the city, on their way to the George Washington Bridge, then to New Jersey, then Delaware – on their way to South Carolina, eventually – and they had begged enough money to enjoy a breakfast of fried eggs, toast and coffee, which had been the best eggs, toast, and coffee they'd ever eaten.

They had stopped to look in the shop window because, since childhood, they had been addicted to television.

The young man said, 'See, I told you. Reruns of *Let's Make a Deal*. Look at that. Jesus, Monty Hall's giving away a twenty-five-year-old Dodge.'

His wife said, 'It's not a twenty-five-year-old Dodge. It's new. At least it was then.'

'Yeah,' he said. 'I guess.'

This conversation had been designed to give them each a little comfort because it was one they had had in their pre-homeless days. But now it only punctuated their desperation, and so they moved on quickly.

It had been a couple of hours since breakfast, and both of them were starting to grow hungry again. After a few days of homelessness they had tried to ignore hunger pangs, but with little success.

'It's not such a bad face, is it?' Erthmun whispered to Patricia David, who was bending over him and was looking concerned.

'It's a beautiful face, Jack,' she said.

'It doesn't look like the face of a toad?'

'It's a beautiful face,' Patricia repeated. 'Jack, can you get up?' She glanced at the open window. 'I'm going to close that,' she said.

'No, don't!' Erthmun protested.

She hesitated briefly, then stepped over to the

window, and slammed it shut. Erthmun looked confusedly at it.

Patricia put her hands under his arms. 'C'mon,
Jack, we've got to get you out of here and to a
hospital. You may be suffering from hypothermia.'

'I've got . . . a joke,' Erthmun whispered.

'A joke. Sure. Tell it to me on the way to the
hospital, okay?'

'No. Let me tell it to you now.'

She still had her hands under his arms. She thought
he felt very cold beneath his heavy jacket. She let go
of his arms, straightened, looked down at him. She
could see only the back of his head. 'If I let you tell
me the joke,' she asked, 'will you let me take you to
a hospital?'

'To a hospital? Yes,' he whispered.

'Okay. Tell me the joke.'

'It's another word joke, another pun,' he whispered, and turned his head a little so he could see her
out of the corner of his eye.

'Yes. Good,' she said. 'A pun. Tell it to me.'

He turned his head back, fell silent a moment, said,
'I don't remember it. It had to do with . . . classical
music.'

'Classical music?'

'Classical music? Yes.'

'But you don't remember it?'

'Don't remember it? Yes. I don't remember it.'

'Does that mean you'll co-operate with me, now?'

He nodded. 'Now? Yes.'

'Good.' She put her hands under his arms again to help him up.

He shook his head. 'No. I remember the joke, now.'

'Jack, for Christ's sake, this really is not the time for jokes.'

'It is,' he whispered. 'Of course it is,' he protested, turned his head and looked pleadingly at her. 'Who tells jokes, Patricia?'

'Huh?'

'*People* tell jokes. *People* tell jokes! Let me tell you mine. Then I'll go wherever you want me to go.'

Before their homelessness, the young couple had read both the *New York Times* and the *Post* religiously. It had seemed to be a necessary part of living in society. They had both kept up with politics and social issues, and they had read the comics page, too, and the sports pages. He had liked baseball and football. She had liked tennis and auto racing.

They no longer read newspapers. It didn't seem necessary because they didn't feel that they were a part of society, any more. They felt that society had rejected them, had spat them out.

If they had continued reading newspapers, they would have seen news about the second massive storm in less than a week that was heading through New York State, driven by fierce Arctic winds. And so, when the temperature dropped precipitously, and the winds picked up, and the snow started, and when the young man's trick knee began to ache, it was their first hint that they were in trouble, that their plan to make it to the George Washington Bridge today would have to be postponed. That they'd have to find some kind of shelter quickly.

They were on East 161st Street. The Harlem river was not far to the west. To the east, a row of sad brownstones stood empty. This, they decided, was their salvation.

'Here's the joke,' Erthmun declared. He had begun shivering. It wasn't continuous – it came and went – and Patricia didn't know if this was a good or bad sign.

'Yes, the joke,' Patricia coaxed. 'Go ahead.' She was still standing behind him. Snow had started to pelt the window with a random tap-tap-tap.

Erthmun sighed, shivered. 'Classical music,' he said. 'Classical music,' he repeated. 'Do you know about classical music? Patricia, do you know about classical music?' He was slurring his words now and Patricia thought that this was a bad sign. 'Yes, I know about classical music, Jack.' It was a lie. She wanted to get him moving.

'Yes,' he said, repeated, 'classical music,' and added quickly, 'What did the . . .' He stopped.

'What did the . . . what?' Patricia coaxed.

'What did the . . . shape-shifting classical composer . . . What did the shape-shifting classical composer . . .' He stopped. He was slurring his words badly now. Patricia could hardly understand him.

'What did the shape-shifting classical composer . . . what?' she coaxed.

'Say?' Erthmun said.

'Say?' Patricia asked.

'Say?' Erthmun repeated.

'Jack, this is—'

'What did the shape-shifting classical composer say?'

'I don't know.'

Erthmun said nothing.

'Can we go, now, Jack?'

'What did the shape-shifting classical composer—'

'I don't know.'

'He said this. He said, "I'm—"' He stopped, shivered, shook. 'He said this, Patricia. He said, "I'm Haydn now, but I'll be Bach later."'

Patricia laughed quickly.

'I'm Haydn now, but I'll be Bach later,' Erthmun repeated.

Patricia said, 'It's funny, Jack. Can we go now?'

'Funny?' Erthmun pleaded. 'Is it? Is it funny, Patricia?'

She hadn't understood him. She said, 'Jack, I can't understand you. You're slurring your words.'

'Is it funny?' he repeated, emphasizing each word.

She understood him. She said, 'It is, Jack. It's funny. Didn't I laugh?'

He said nothing. He shivered again.

'Didn't I laugh?' Patricia repeated.

'Laugh?' Erthmun said. 'Yes.'

'And we can go now?'

'Go now? Yes,' Erthmun managed. 'I think we should go now.'

Breaking into one of the abandoned brownstones hadn't been as easy as the homeless couple had imagined. They had chosen one whose door was still planked shut because the others, they decided, were probably filled with druggies and other homeless people. But getting the plank off the door was no easy matter. The young man had thought he could simply pull it loose by hand, but it had been nailed into the oak door frame with huge nails, and though he and his wife both tried, they soon realized that pulling the plank loose without some kind of lever would be impossible.

He told her to wait on the front steps while he went looking for something with which to prise the plank loose. The snow, by then, had begun curling around them like a cloud, and the wind was painfully cold, so she agreed to wait for him in a little sheltered area to the right of the door.

He looked in the storm for quite a while. At last, he found an abandoned car whose trunk wasn't latched securely. He located a tyre iron in the trunk – this was a providential find, he decided – made his way through the storm back to the brownstone and pried the plank loose from the front door. This was a chore that made his hands ache from exposure to the cold wind, and his arms ache from the effort, so when he was done, he cursed into the storm and threw the tyre iron away in anger.

The inside of the brownstone was a place of devastation. A stairway that had once led to the second floor was gone. A homemade wooden ladder stood in its place. Much of the first floor was missing, revealing a basement full of litter and dust. Above, snow was making its way through what could only have been a hole in the roof, down a short hallway, and then over the landing.

The young woman said, 'This is an awful place.'

Her husband agreed.

They decided that, as soon as possible, they would leave. But, for now, it was their only shelter.

They climbed the homemade ladder to the second floor.

Thirty-one

In the Adirondacks

The rabbit knew nothing about death. It had lived for ever, it would continue to live for ever. Still, there were the predators. The fox, the great horned owl, the red-tailed hawk. And the others.

Instinct did not tell the rabbit that its enemies required its death, only that its flesh would make a satisfying meal. So, when the rabbit's lungs refused to work because its throat had been crushed, it slid into death not as frantically as its killer might. No memories or sympathies crowded back. Its eyes opened wide, its always-twitching nose stopped twitching, its muscles tensed – as if readying themselves for use – and it died.

Then its body was carried away by the ears for use as food. And its killer was neither joyful nor saddened because of the killing. Its killer had been beset by hunger and cold and a craving for meat. And the rabbit had not been as cautious as it could have been.

Thirty-two

Erthmun dreamed of running. He dreamed that the tall golden grasses moving past him as he ran coalesced into one monolithic golden form because he was running so fast. He dreamed that the sun raced him through the day, and that he outran the noises of insects and birds, and he saw other insects and other birds in a blur, trying in vain to flutter out of his way. But he was Death, and he was Life, and nothing could get out of his way, and nothing could stop him.

It was a wonderful dream, and he did not wake from it at once.

Patricia David said, 'He's smiling.'

The doctor standing with her at Erthmun's bedside said, 'A dream.'

'I know,' said Patricia David. 'I assume that's a good sign.'

The doctor shook her head a little. 'It's a dream, that's all.'

In the empty brownstone on East 161st Street, the young homeless couple had busied themselves with talk of architecture because they were trying to ignore their hunger pangs, their desperation, and the storm that had worked into an urban fury beyond the tall windows. Most of these windows were cracked, though none on the second floor were broken, and some had been covered with plywood that, oddly, still smelled of glue and formaldehyde, and still bore a fresh, orange cast.

The young man had said, 'They don't make houses like this any more.'

The young woman had agreed, and then announced that it was a federal-style house, to which the young man chortled and said that of course it wasn't a federal-style house, it was late Victorian.

There were four rooms on the second floor. They were of a uniform size – large enough for a double bed and a couple of dressers, though the rooms were empty now – and each had a small closet with a closed door. The young couple had not looked into any of the closets because their curiosity was not at peak today, and because they did not imagine there was anything in them that they wanted to see, or which would be useful.

There was also a bathroom, *sans* fixtures except for a water-stained oak medicine cabinet with a cracked mirror. All the walls had been done in a bold, blue-flower print wallpaper that was remarkably well preserved though water-stained, too, and the floors were hardwood, covered with a fine grey dust, which was undisturbed; the young couple had accepted that this was a good sign.

They were huddled together in a room that was protected from the direct onslaught of the wind and so was a few degrees warmer than the other rooms. The young man said, 'It usually doesn't get this cold in New York.'

'But it gets real hot in the summer,' the young woman said.

'I wish it was summer now,' said the young man.

They fell silent after that. They maintained silence for quite a long while. They did not want to believe that the storm was intensifying, although this was obvious from the whining noise it made against the window glass. They didn't want to admit, either, that the day was ending, that the pale light in the house was beginning to fade. Cold, darkness and hunger in such a place as this were not what they had planned for themselves a year earlier. They had planned babies, mortgages, car payments, barbecues on balconies that overlooked Central Park.

Erthmun's dream of running ended and became a dream of disease. He saw the earth beneath his feet

rise up in great globular pustules that ran with putrefaction and partly coagulated blood, which clogged
the mouths of living things around him – insects,
animals, birds, people at play – made them gasp for
air and fall dead. Then they became globular pustules
that ran with putrefaction and coagulates that clogged
open mouths; these open mouths appeared from the
earth around him, from within mounds of fallen
leaves and punctured mushrooms and flower petals.
These open mouths became open eyes, which were
sky-blue, and they quickly became clouded with
coagulates. Then there were faces in the earth, open
rosebud mouths and open sky-blue eyes and noses
clogged with coagulates and clumps of earth.

Then the earth was alive with dark creatures that
ran naked through golden grass and mounted one
another and laughed and ate and ate and ate, and
mounted one another, and mounted one another,
and watched the air change and the living things
sleep, and dream, and die, and died themselves.

And the earth was a place of disease and cold and
death. And Erthmun himself was running naked in
this place, and his bare feet plunged into hip-deep
snow, and he leaped through it as if he were weight-
less. Then it caught him, held him, clogged his mouth,
his nose, clouded his eyes, became warm, became
clumps of wet, warm earth, became great globular
pustules that spouted partly coagulated blood and
putrefaction, and then there were mouths in the
putrefaction, mouths spitting out the coagulates,

mouths screaming, mouths crying, 'I'm human! I'm human!'

'My God!' breathed Patricia David.

'Mr Erthmun,' said the doctor, who had been standing by the bedside with her – she was shaking Jack, now, trying to rouse him. 'Wake up, Mr Erthmun! Wake up!'

'Jack?' Patricia whispered.

The young woman, whose name was Greta, felt delicious, real, alive. She felt as if she could jump from her fifth-floor window and land unscathed in the Park and then run for hours and hours without losing breath. She thought that she had once done just that sort of thing, but in a different place. Not her childhood home in Pennsylvania, but some other home. She tried to remember it. She saw trees and hills in her mind's eye, and the name of the place itself tickled and teased her memory but stayed just out of reach.

Five storeys below, at Columbus Circle, she could see that some of the police cars were leaving. She thought again that she was somehow responsible for what they had been doing in the Park, but when she tried to recall exactly how she could have been responsible, she got only a sense of quick desperation, and then a feeling of orgasmic satisfaction. It was very stimulating, so she tried to tweak the memory often as she sat at her window. If she had cared to look, she would have seen her dim reflection in the window glass, would have seen her quivering smile come and go as if in time with her inhales and exhales. And, not for the first time, she would have wondered just what sort of creature she was.

Thirty-three

Ten thousand living things had made a home of the brownstone on East 161st Street. Jumping spiders, silverfish, brown German cockroaches, termites, fleas, mice, rats, lice. And two human beings removed from their place in society by unfortunate events.

There was another in the brownstone, too. She had been displaced and destroyed by humans in times past, and then had been remade the same as she had been, much the way the earth remakes a carrot, or a head of lettuce, or a burying beetle.

The homeless young woman said that she was depressed, and her husband said that he was depressed, too, but who could blame them? Christ, here they were, in a shitty abandoned brownstone in a shitty part of New York City, on a shitty day when they couldn't go anywhere even if they wanted to, and it

was goddamned cold, besides, and they were both
goddamned hungry – *Gee, wouldn't a steak be nice . . .*

'Enough!' said the young woman.

'Sorry,' said her husband.

'Enough,' she said again, more quietly, with
resolve. 'I have had enough. I'm not depressed, or
sad, or any of that shit. I have just *had enough*!'

'I understand.'

'I don't even want you to understand. I don't want
anything. I don't want a steak, or a TV, or a fucking
bus ticket to South Carolina, or any of that stuff. I
don't even want a bed to sleep in, or a nice pillow, or
a fucking pet hamster! None of that stuff means
anything because you lose it all, anyway. It all gets
taken away from you. You try to hold on to it, and it
all gets taken away. Jesus! I have just had *enough*!'

'I know. I'm sorry.'

She didn't look at him. It would have been difficult
for him to see her if she had looked at him, because
the light had grown dim in the room. As its two tall
windows had been boarded over the only light was a
rectangle of soft, blue green phosphorescence at the
doorway; this was light that the storm had let in from
the city around them, and it was so dim that they
could not see it unless they looked obliquely at it, just
as they might have seen a dim star on a clear night.

'I don't like you feeling this way,' the young man
said.

His wife said nothing.

'Things will work out, you'll see. We'll just stay

here tonight, and tomorrow we'll go and . . . hell, we can get some day jobs, and we can stay here for a couple of nights, if we need to, as long as we're trying to save money—'

'Shut up!' whispered the young woman.

'Yeah, sure, I'm sorry,' said the young man.

He put his arm around her. She did not protest at this, but neither did she lean into him for warmth, or affection. He said, 'Don't give up.'

But she said nothing.

The other creatures sharing the brownstone were not interested in much besides warmth, except for the termites who, *en masse*, generated their own heat within the wood in the house as they made an extended meal of the place. The cockroaches congregated in another part of the building, where there was plenty to eat, and the jumping spiders – there were four in the house – spent their time huddled in corners, legs tight around their little dark bodies, and their senses alert to the errant fly or spider mite or flea. It was a brutal existence for everything in the house. Lives ended and lives began cyclically, just as in the universe beyond the house, and in the earth itself, in the plant life that sprang from the earth, in the insects that fed on the plant life, and in the birds that fed on the insects.

'Listen,' said the young man. 'I know you don't want me to talk to you. I know you want me to shut up.

But is it all right if I just . . . talk? You don't have to listen.'

His wife said nothing. She was tense under his arm. He could feel her breathing, though the noises of the storm covered the sounds of her breathing.

'Okay,' said the young man. 'I'll talk.' And he did. He kept his eyes on her and he talked to her for a long, long while. He told her about how he was going to get them out of their crummy situation. He told her that he was going to go back to college and get a teaching certificate and get a job at a high school. He told her that he'd teach something, maybe gym, and then he'd get tenured, so they couldn't fire him, and if they couldn't fire him, then their future was pretty secure, they wouldn't have to worry a lot about money, and they could have kids. And when he stopped talking for a moment, and looked away from her – his eyes had adjusted to the dim light and he could see her profile; it was grey against the darkness – and towards the blue-green phosphorescence that was the doorway, he saw that someone was standing in it, hunched over, hands on the doorjamb, legs wide.

And he screamed.

Erthmun said, 'I don't know.' He closed his eyes, looked as if he were in pain.

The doctor said, 'Mr Erthmun, perhaps it's best if you sleep.'

'I've *been* asleep, dammit!' He opened his eyes. He

sighed, looked at the doctor. 'I've been asleep,' he repeated. 'I don't need to sleep.' He closed his eyes again, opened them, looked first at Patricia, then at the doctor. 'What is this place?' he asked.

'You're in a hospital, Jack,' Patricia told him.

'You're suffering from hypothermia,' the doctor said.

'Hypothermia,' Erthmun said, though simply as an echo to what the doctor had said.

'You're going to be all right,' Patricia told him. 'You need to rest.'

'What is this place?' he asked again.

'A hospital.'

'Hospital,' Erthmun echoed. 'Hypothermia.' He closed his eyes, opened them, stared at the ceiling. 'I dreamed,' he whispered, as if to no one in particular. 'I never dream. But I dreamed.'

'Mr Erthmun, it was a nightmare,' the doctor said. 'But you're awake, now.'

'I don't have nightmares,' Erthmun said. 'I don't dream.'

'We all dream,' said the doctor.

'I don't know,' said Erthmun, and his eyes were still on the ceiling.

'What don't you know, Jack?' Patricia asked.

He said nothing.

'Jack?' she coaxed.

He said nothing.

Thirty-four

And when he was done screaming, the young home-less man saw that the thing standing in the doorway was gone, and he could feel that his wife was clinging to him so tightly that it hurt.

After several minutes, he said, 'I saw something.'

His wife said nothing. She still clung to him. He put his hand comfortingly on hers. 'I saw something,' he repeated. 'I screamed because I saw something.' He hesitated, played back the moment, saw again in his mind's eye the thing standing in the rectangle of soft blue-green phosphorescence that was the doorway. He continued, 'I thought I saw something.' He nodded to indicate the doorway. 'There.' He paused. 'But maybe I didn't.' He patted her hand, thought it was a stupid gesture under the circumstances, said, 'It's all right. There's no one in the house but us. How would they get in? They couldn't get in.' He paused. 'We're the only ones here.'

His wife clung silently to him.

Greta liked chocolate. She thought that she had always liked chocolate. She thought she remembered stuffing gobs of it in her mouth when she was a child and telling her mother – whom she remembered looking on with an odd mixture of horror and rebuke – 'It's better than mud', which she thought made her mother's look of horror and rebuke become one of perplexity.

Greta was eating chocolate now. It wasn't cheap chocolate. It wasn't mud. It wasn't Hershey's, or Nestlé's Crunch. It was lovely chocolate. Godiva. Perugina. Chocolate that was sex and sensuality. Chocolate that was life itself. Chocolate that filled her soul. Chocolate that made her moist, and made her eyes close, and made her senses quiver.

Greta was surprised at this new creature that had emerged from within the Greta she had known for so long. And she was delighted, too. This Greta would not sit longingly for hours at her window and do nothing. This Greta had enough life in her to do what that other Greta was afraid to do.

Breathe!

Be!

The doctor said to Patricia David, 'He is clearly experiencing some disorientation. It's not unusual in cases of hypothermia. But he's no longer in any danger. I'd say it was fortunate that you got him here as soon as you did, otherwise this whole scenario might have played out very differently.'

Erthmun was asleep. He was on his back and he was breathing lightly. Patricia had supposed that he was a man who snored. But he didn't snore. He slept as silently as stone.

Patricia said, 'So you think he'll be able to go home in a day or two?'

'There's no reason that he can't go home tomorrow,' the doctor said.

'Tomorrow? That's good.'

'We'll just keep him here tonight as a precautionary measure, and he can go home tomorrow.'

'Yes,' Patricia said. 'He'll like that.'

In the brownstone on East 161st Street, the young homeless man felt trapped by the storm, trapped by his homelessness, trapped by the sudden, silent and motionless panic of his wife. Trapped by the other thing in the house that had appeared so briefly, and now waited for them somewhere beyond the tall rectangle of soft, blue-green phosphorescence that was the doorway.

He said, 'C'mon, babe, we've got to get out of here, I think.' He had said the same words to her a half-dozen times in the past fifteen minutes, but with no response. She continued clinging to him; she was still hurting his arm with her incredibly strong grip, and

he imagined that he'd have finger-shaped bruises on
that arm before long.

He said now, 'What are we going to do?'

She said nothing.

'If we don't get out of here, this is it,' he said.

Silence. Beyond the house, the storm droned on.
He thought it sounded like laughter.

Thirty-five

These weren't dreams. How could they be dreams? He could smell the tangy odour of wet earth, freshly washed clothes, his father's aftershave, a breakfast just eaten.

He didn't dream.

He never dreamed.

How could this be a dream?

Because his mother was here, too, and his sisters, and his house – although it existed only as a dark, windowless box at the horizon – and the golden grasses swaying like flowers, and the insects that tried to get out of his way, the crickets, the mantises, the garden spiders retreating deep into their webs.

And the others.

Those who shadowed him, and ran with him, who made the most of their time, just as he was doing, who made the most of what the earth had given them, just as he was doing.

His mother would have been amazed if she had seen him run like this. His father, too. And his sisters. All amazed. *Look at that little fireplug run!* they would have said. *Who would have known he could run like that?*

Who?

Only the others. Those who shadowed him and ran with him and mimicked his laughter, and felt his joy.

The others. They were the only ones who existed here. There were no murder victims in this place, in these high hills and golden fields. There were no men with wounds and mouths agape. There were no women who had been made to look foolish.

There was only the dark, windowless box that was his house, far off, at the horizon. Only the golden grasses.

Only the others.

And him.

And the other child. The one he had found playing with a doll at a stream far from the house; the one who told him her name was Greta, and whom he had found spooning mud into the mouth of her doll.

'Why are you doing that?' he asked.

'Doing that?' echoed the girl. 'It's chocolate. I like chocolate. My doll likes chocolate.'

'I like chocolate, too,' he said.

'Chocolate, too,' she echoed. 'And do you like my doll's eyes?'

'Doll's eyes,' he said, and looked closely at it. It was

a naked, plastic doll; its eyes had been plucked out and crumpled bright green paper put in their place.

He asked, 'Why'd you do that?'

'Do that?' she echoed. 'I like green. Don't you like green? I like chocolate and I like things that are green.'

'I like green,' he said.

'I like green,' she echoed.

'This is what I'm going to do, babe,' said the young homeless man to his wife. 'I'm going to leave you here . . .' she clung even more tightly to him '. . . I'm going to leave you here, and I'm going to go just over there,' he nodded at the doorway, 'and then I'll come right back.' She continued clinging to him. He took hold of her hand, tried to pry her fingers free. He pleaded, 'You've got to let go of me, babe.' He pulled hard on her fingers, hoped he wasn't hurting her, got her hand free, let go of it; she grabbed his arm again, even tighter.

'Babe,' he said, 'this is stupid. We don't want to die here, do we?'

Nothing.

'Do we?' he said again.

Nothing.

He lurched away from her, suddenly. It was for her own good, he told himself. At this point, she was her own worst enemy. Better a little pain now than death later.

He stood unsteadily, because his legs had gone to

sleep, wobbled a bit, looked down at her. She was a yellowish mass near his feet. He thought she was looking up at him. 'I'm going over there,' he said, and moved his arm a little to indicate the doorway.

She said nothing.

'Okay?' he said.

Nothing.

He thought that he needed a weapon. But what was there? The room was empty.

Something in the closet, maybe. Where was it? He looked about. He saw a dark rectangle against the far wall. Surely that was the closet door.

'I'm going over there,' he said. 'I'm going to go and look in the closet.'

'No,' she whispered.

He was happy that at last she'd spoken. 'I have to,' he said.

'Why?' she said.

'I need some kind of weapon. I have to look in the closet.'

'Don't!' she said.

'I have to,' he said again. He thought that he was becoming angry with her.

She said nothing.

He crossed slowly to the dark rectangle he supposed was the closet door. He hoped that as he drew closer to it he would be able to see it better. But that didn't happen. It was in a darker area of the room, well away from the door and the soft blue-green phos-phorescence, and as he drew closer to the dark rectangle it merely became darker, and monolithic. When he was close to it, he reached into the area where the doorknob should have been. His fingers touched cold wood. He lowered his hand a little. His fingers touched colder metal. He probed it, found a small hole in it, whispered, 'Shit.' No doorknob.

'Don't!' he heard from behind him.

'I have to,' he said yet again.

'Don't!' he heard.

'It's all right, babe,' he said.

'Don't!' he heard.

He began to speak, and heard, from the middle of the dark room, in his own voice, 'It's all right, babe.'

He whirled about.

He saw the dark oval of a face near his, the darker ovals of eyes on him, the oval of a mouth wide open.

Thirty-six

Then it was gone. And he saw that his wife was standing between him and the doorway.

She said, her voice shaking and weak, 'What was it?'

He said nothing. He had backed reflexively away and now was standing with his rear-end to the closet door and his legs quivering. He thought that he had peed his pants.

'What was it?' his wife said again. 'Dammit, what was that thing?' Her voice had become stronger, firmer.

The young man said, 'I . . . don't know.'

'You don't know?' she shrieked. 'You don't fucking *know*?' She came quickly forward. 'For Christ's sake, why *don't* you know? Why in the hell don't you know?' She was standing directly in front of him, now. 'You bring me here, you bring me here to this goddamned place and you don't fucking know what *lives* here? That's fucking stupid! *You're* fucking stupid!' She put her hands flat on his chest and pushed against him, but he went nowhere because he was standing against the closet door. She shrieked at him, 'I'm going to *die* here, for Christ's sake, and you don't know *why*? Why *don't* you know, why *don't* you know?' She pummelled his chest with her fists. 'It's up to you to *know*! You're my *husband*, you *have* to know! You have to know!'

He let her pummel him. She wasn't hurting him much, and he thought he deserved whatever pain she could inflict. Because she was going to die, it was obvious. And so was he. What could they do about it? They were trapped, by the storm, by their home-lessness, by the thing that shared this place with them, by hunger.

In the house on Four Mile Creek, the same moment

They were like termites in the house. They huddled together in corners in its many rooms. And if a person had been listening to them, that person would have heard what sounded like a deep, throaty, purring noise – throats responding to the quivering that kept them warm, that produced heat and kept them alive in this place where huddling together was the only way to contain heat.

Occasionally, amid this purring, a listener might

have heard words, too. The voice of a male, and the voice of a female. A listener would have heard, 'Do you think this is safe?' and 'Okay, so what do we do now? Spread our sleeping bags out here?' and 'Maybe there's a fireplace,' and 'Inner room where?'

In this month, under this desperation, these creatures had no idea what such words meant. They had heard the words, and they were repeating them. They repeated much. They loved the sounds they heard. They repeated the sounds of animals, too, and insects and birds. In summer, a listener might be walking in a meadow and hear what he supposed were only the many and varied sounds of the meadow. And, after a fashion, he would be right.

But this month, under this desperation, these creatures quivered for warmth, and sounds came from them involuntarily, like the grunting of bears on lazy strolls. And the twitterings of insects, too, the raucous cries of bluejays, a human conversation born of fear and impending panic.

Under their desperation, these naked forms knew nothing of time and everything of cold, which was death. And so they huddled together in the corners in all the rooms of the big house, and the noises that came from the house were like the noises of meadows and conversations, sleeping cats and strolling bears.

The homeless man's wife had done what the man thought was a very stupid thing, though he couldn't blame her for it. She had run from him, out of the room, into the hallway, and then, in the dark, had blundered over the place where the stairs should have been. Now she lay groaning somewhere below him; the young man wasn't sure if she was on the first floor or beneath that in the cellar – he could see her only dimly. And he was trying to imagine how he would reach her, because, in her fall, she had knocked over the home-made ladder.

He called to her, 'Are you all right?' but she only groaned in response, and he tried to convince himself that this was a good sign, really – at least she could groan – and he repeated, 'Are you all right?' though he knew that she wasn't. How could she be? She'd fallen ... what? ... fifteen, twenty feet in the pitch dark, in the cold, and only God knew what she might have fallen on or what bones she might have broken. He imagined her lying in pain and in terrified resignation about her own death, and it tore him apart because he loved her, and because he had loved the life they had once planned to live.

'I'm coming down there, babe,' he called. And he knew that this was true. He really *was* going down there, to where she lay. He simply didn't know how he was going to do it.

When Erthmun woke he saw black and white floor tiles, beige walls, shadowless fluorescent light, and he smelled antiseptic, blood, freshly cooked eggs, and he heard people talking at a distance – 'Look what Karen brought you, darling. Isn't it sweet?' and, from another place, 'He says it's not a problem and that we have nothing to worry about.'

Erthmun sighed. No high hills and golden grasses in this place. No crickets hopping out of his way.

This was the place of the grinning dead.

Thirty-seven

Morning in Manhattan

It had been a bad night for the homeless man. What could he do? It was too dark to find his way down to his wife, who had groaned for hours, and was now silent. He could see her, though not clearly because the storm was robbing the morning sunlight. He saw her as if through a fog. He saw that she was on her back in the cellar and that her arms and legs were spread wide. He couldn't see her face. He wasn't sure that he wanted to see it.

And the storm had lashed the brownstone all night, too, which had been maddening for a couple of reasons, not the least of which was that he hadn't been able to *hear* anything beyond his wife's groaning, which had been as loud as a scream, and was clearly the result of terrible pain. But he hadn't been able to hear anything else, hadn't been able to hear if

something were moving towards him from somewhere within one of the bedrooms. So he had sat
with his all-but-blind gaze on the second-floor
interior of the brownstone, and had listened to the
screams of the storm and the screaming groans of his
wife, and he had prayed for morning.

The doctor said, 'He checked out, Miss David.'
   'When?' Patricia asked.
   'About a half-hour ago, I think.'
   'Just like that?'
   'Of course. We have no right to keep him here.'
   'Do you know where he went?'
   'My assumption is that he went home.'
   'Thanks,' Patricia said, and hung up.

Erthmun was like many New Yorkers: he didn't own
a car. It was too much of a hassle to keep one parked
and secure. You paid as much a month to park a car
in a secure garage as many people outside the city
paid for a mortgage. And if you parked on the street
– assuming you could find an empty parking space –
the chances were more than even that you'd wake in
the morning and find that the car had been stripped
of everything except its gas tank and brake pedal. So,
at work, he used his unmarked police car, which he
turned in at the end of his shift and took a bus home
or walked.

   This morning, there were no buses, only a few
taxis, and even fewer private cars moving on the

streets of Manhattan. The snow was knee-deep on many of the side streets, and on the main streets – Broadway, Lexington, Fifth Avenue, Madison – ploughs were trying gamely to bring the city back to some semblance of normality. But it was impossible because storms of this magnitude were a once-in-a-decade occurrence here, and no one knew how to deal with them properly. The city had come to a standstill.

He found a little deli called Marty's on 32nd Street. It was empty except for the owner, who was standing behind the counter in a white T-shirt and white apron and looking glumly at the storm beyond his windows.

Erthmun went into the deli. 'Jesus, mister,' the owner said to him, 'what the hell are you doin' out there?'

Erthmun sat at the counter. It was a highly polished pale green and squeaky clean; there were ketchup bottles and little metal baskets filled with Equal packets placed neatly every couple of feet along it. 'Dying, I think,' Erthmun said. He folded his hands in front of him, noted their reflection in the counter top, saw that they were shaking.

The owner of the deli smiled and said, 'Ain't we all, huh?'

Erthmun nodded.

'Ain't we all dyin'?' the owner repeated, and then announced that he was Marty himself, and extended his hand. Erthmun stared at it a moment, then lifted

his own quivering hand. 'Tell me you ain't a cop,'
Marty said.

Erthmun said, 'I'm a cop.'

'I know cops,' Marty said, grinning. He had a round
face, big, oval dark eyes, and his grin was pleasant
and non-judgemental. 'I been servin' cops here for
twenty-five years, huh. Coffee?'

Erthmun said, 'Coffee? Yes.'

Marty gave him a concerned look. 'You okay?'

'I'm okay.'

'You don't seem okay. Maybe you need more than
coffee, huh?'

'No, just coffee.' Erthmun could feel that he was
shaking now. He thought that in the recent past he
had felt the same way that he was feeling now, and
that it had not boded well for him. He added, 'Have I
been in here before, Marty?'

'I don't think so,' Marty said, and put a big, cream-
coloured mug full of pitch black coffee in front of
Erthmun. 'But who can say? What, you don't
remember?'

Erthmun shook his head, sipped his coffee and
spilled some on the counter because his hands were
shaking. Marty mopped up the spill immediately with
a towel.

Erthmun sipped his coffee again. He thought that
he was being very noisy about it, and he apologized.

Marty said, 'Every morning I got fifty noisy sippers
in here. It's like music.' He grinned again.

Erthmun said, 'I'm being stalked. I'm being hunted.'

Marty said nothing.

Erthmun sipped his coffee.

Marty said, as if concerned, 'Who's stalking you?'

Erthmun said, 'It could be anyone.' He realized that he was shaking badly, now, and that it was affecting his speech. He thought that he sounded like a fool, but these were such important things to say. 'It could be you. It could be anyone. It could be Helen.'

'It ain't me,' Marty said.

'It could be Helen,' Erthmun repeated. 'Do you know her? Do you know her?'

'Who?'

'Helen.'

'No. I don't know no Helen.'

'Who does? Who does? She's like . . . she's like a puff of . . . smoke, Marty. Smoke. She's like smoke. Do you know her?'

'No,' Marty said again.

'Who knows her?' Erthmun said. 'I don't.'

'Sure,' said Marty. He was getting nervous.

'She could be you, or me, or anyone,' Erthmun said. 'But she isn't. She isn't. She's . . . Helen. And she does what she does!'

'Sure,' Marty repeated.

'She eats,' Erthmun said. 'We all eat.'

'We do, sure we do. We eat,' Marty said.

'I don't know,' Erthmun said. 'I met someone once. A long, long time ago, in another place. But she wasn't Helen. Only Helen is Helen. Helen isn't me, or you.'

'Maybe you'd like your coffee warmed up?' Marty asked.

'But she could be you and you wouldn't know it,' Erthmun said.

'You're shakin' real bad, mister,' Marty said. 'I can't understand what you're sayin'.'

'You don't need to,' Erthmun said. He set his cup down hard, so more coffee sloshed onto the counter. Marty did not step forward to clean it up.

'Jesus!' Erthmun shouted.

Marty lurched.

'It could be you! It could be you!' Erthmun shouted. 'Why did I come in here?' The energy of his sudden anger was overcoming the fact that he was cold and shaking, and his words were easier to understand, now. 'Did you *invite* me in here?'

'You came in here all on your own,' Marty said.

'Did I? Why would I do that?'

'I guess to get some coffee,' Marty said.

'Are you *human*?' Erthmun shouted. 'Are you *human*?'

'Sure I'm human.'

'But do you *know*? Can you prove it? No. Who knows? Can you reach back and pull yourself out of your mother's womb and say, *"This is me, and I'm human"*? No. Who can? No one. Do you realize that there are dead women with chocolate stuffed in their mouths in this city right now as we speak? Think of it. Think of it! Chocolate in their mouths! Naked, dead women with chocolate in their mouths and no one knows why! Do *you* know why? No. No one knows! These are *previous* women!'

'Sure,' said Marty. He was backing away as Erthmun ranted.

Erthmun said, 'Women who are no more than soil, no more than the earth itself, women who are like plastic dolls, women will never taste the chocolate that fills their mouths!'

'Sure,' said Marty.

'And what do you know, Marty? Can you reach into your mother's womb, can you go back in time and reach into your mother's womb and say, "*Yes this is me, and this is my father who fucked my mother one night who fucked her sweetly and said he loved her when he was done, and put his seed into her, and it was* that *seed that made me.*" And can you say, "*And this is my mother, whose womb I'm in*"? You can't say any of that. You can't say any of it!'

Erthmun stood suddenly; Marty lurched. There was a small handgun beneath the counter not far from him.

Erthmun said, 'It is these women who are stalking me!'

'Sure,' said Marty, bent over, and put his hand on the gun beneath the counter.

'What's that?' Erthmun said. 'What are you doing?'

'Nothing,' said Marty.

'Good,' said Erthmun.

*

At that moment, Patricia was trying to telephone him from her cellular phone. She was in her car which was stuck in snow near the corner of Lexington and 37th Street. There were others stuck around her; most had been abandoned, but a few drivers were furiously trying to get their vehicles moving.

She let Erthmun's number ring a couple of dozen times.

The homeless man could see well enough now, and he thought that his wife was dead. He could see her eyes, and they were closed. He could see her mouth, and he thought that it was open a little. He didn't think that her chest was moving at all. She lay directly beneath him, in the cellar, her legs and arms splayed out.

He wondered if he could jump from here to the first floor. It was only a little further, he guessed, than if he stood with his arm straight up. It wasn't twenty feet, as he had first thought. It was fifteen feet, tops – not a whole bunch more than the distance from a basketball hoop to the ground. He could jump it. He could do it, and when he had done it it would be done and he wouldn't have to think about it any more. It would be behind him. He'd be on the first floor, and he'd be able to tell if his wife was dead. And if she wasn't . . . What then? What was he going to do then? Carry her somewhere? Carry her to a hospital? Go and call an ambulance. How would he pay for it, because for sure they'd want him to pay for it. He didn't even know the address here. *A brownstone on East 161st Street.* Is that what he'd say? *And how are you going to pay for this ambulance?* they'd say. He'd have no answer.

He stared at his wife. He hoped to see that her chest was moving a little, that her lips were spluttering – though, if they were, he realized, he wouldn't be able to see it from here – or that her eyes would open.

He wanted her to live.

He wanted them both to live.

Christ, he was hungry!

Thirty-eight

Morning at the house on Four Mile Creek
Sunlight fell on some of the creatures huddled in a corner in that house. It was like a salve, a healing potion. They had watched it creep across the floor towards them as morning started. They had known what it was, and that its very touch brought wonderful pleasure and warmth. But they didn't move to greet it. No one got up from the naked heap and moved across the floor to greet it. This would have taken heat away from the others and would have brought cold and pain to the individual who did it. Better to wait for the sunlight together, as one.

The sunlight touched a few of them at the feet, though not all of them, and when this happened, all groaned in pleasure because all could feel the sunlight through the ones it touched.

He was still bent over, still had his hand on the butt of the gun. He could see the other man's eyes on him, and he could read no threat or danger in them. But the man was so odd with his talk of naked women and chocolate and stalkers. The man was crazy, sure, and crazy people did crazy things, unless they were stopped.

Erthmun said, 'I don't have a gun. Did you believe that I had a gun?'

Marty said, 'I want you just to leave, huh?'

'I'm cold,' Erthmun told him.

Marty gripped the gun, straightened with it in his hand, but kept it pointed at the floor.

Erthmun said, 'Would you shoot another human being?'

'I don't know if I ever would shoot anybody,' Marty said.

'I'm another human being,' Erthmun said. 'I'm another human being,' he repeated. 'And I'm cold. I need to be here.'

'I don't think you can stay in my delicatessen,' Marty said. His words alone would have indicated uncertainty but his tone was firm. 'I have the gun and I don't know what I would do with it. I think that you should go to the hospital.'

Erthmun pointed stiffly to indicate the street and the storm. He said, his voice quaking again, 'Do you see that?'

'I see it,' Marty said.

'If I leave here, that storm will kill me,' Erthmun said.

Marty shook his head. 'No. Not in this city. There are places for you to go. So I want you to leave and go to one of those places. Go to Penn station. It's not far. It's warm. Go there.'

Erthmun stared at the man for a long moment. These words went through Erthmun's head: *What's happening to me? What do I know? Why am I here, in this city, in this restaurant? Why does that man have a gun in his hand? What does he want to do with it? What am I? What am I?*

As quietly and as gracefully as a moth opening its wings, Helen had stepped out of the near-dark in the cellar of the brownstone on East 161st Street, and now she stood naked and incredible in the dim morning light, dark hair streaming down her back, her sky-blue eyes fixed on the homeless man above her, on the second floor, as if she were mentally weighing his worth to her. And he stared back in awe, because he knew that this was the incredible creature that had haunted him the previous evening.

Under other circumstances, the homeless man would have thought, She's naked, she's a woman – she's vulnerable. But these were not such circumstances. This creature was no more vulnerable than the storm that still lashed the house. No more vulnerable than Death itself.

So he stared silently at her. His gaze did not move more than once from her eyes to her body, which was as exquisite as any female body he had seen.

And, still as if assessing his worth to her, she stared silently back. After not too long, she bent quickly over the body of the homeless man's wife, ripped open the woman's grey wool jacket, tore at the blue sweater beneath, and the pink blouse beneath that, and shoved her hand far into the woman's stomach. Then she devoured what she pulled out of that stomach – the woman's small intestine, part of her liver, a kidney – while the homeless man watched silently from above.

'Who the fuck moves that quickly?' Erthmun snarled. 'Who?'

Marty's mouth was open and the nose of his own gun was stuck into it. Erthmun was holding the gun, and he had bent Marty backwards over one of his stoves – which had not been lit. Erthmun was holding the neck of Marty's white shirt tightly in one hand.

A dollop of drool fell from Erthmun's mouth to Marty's neck; this caused Marty to make a little squeaking noise.

'What's that? Erthmun demanded. 'Did you say something to me?'

Marty shook his head a little. He did not want to annoy this man any further. He'd seen him move at a speed no man should be able to move. He thought, upon awed reflection, that the man had even become invisible for a moment because he was moving so fast.

'Do you know this?' Erthmun snarled. 'Do you know this?'

Again, Marty shook his head a little.

'Do you know this?' Erthmun repeated, and Marty got the fleeting impression that Erthmun had no idea that he was asking a question, that the words were simply an echo. Marty shook his head again. Another dollop of drool fell to his neck; he tried to ignore it.

Erthmun said, 'I don't *want* to kill you. I don't *want* to kill you.' Short pause. 'But maybe I *need* to!'

'You don't!' Marty whispered.

'Maybe I do! Maybe I do! How do you know what I have to do? How do you know what I'm compelled to do? You don't know me. Who knows me? You don't!'

Marty said nothing.

Erthmun cocked the gun. 'Maybe I *do* want to kill you! Maybe there's no maybe at all about anything I do. I do what I do because I feel good when I do it. And so I do what I do to feel good, because it's part of being alive. Feeling good is part of being alive. I feel good. You feel good. We do what we do and we feel good. That makes sense. Doesn't that make sense?'

Nothing.

'Answer me, Goddammit! Answer me!'

'Yes,' Marty whispered.

'Do you know me? How can you know me? Who knows me?'

Marty shook his head in terrified confusion.

Erthmun took the gun from the man's mouth, pointed it at the ceiling, fired, fired again, again. Marty's body lurched with each shot.

Erthmun tossed the gun far across the deli. He held his hand up, fingers wide, for Marty to see. 'I don't need that,' he said. 'I have these.'

Thirty-nine

Helen had finished. She was drenched in the blood of the homeless woman, whose eyes had opened in the past few minutes; the woman's husband had dimly noted this from his perch above, and, as dimly, he had ascribed it to some errant reaction of nerves or latent electricity. It did not occur to him for long that his wife had been alive through her own devouring. The idea was monstrous; no one could continue living, or go on believing in an ordered and sane universe, and accept that such a thing had happened to one who is loved.

Helen had finished, had consumed her last meal, had known her last great pleasure.

And now she was dying.

The homeless man did not know this. He saw her move off – with more clumsiness than the quiet grace with which she had made her appearance – into the near-dark on the first floor of the brownstone; her hip-length auburn hair was the last he saw of her. And as he stared at his disembowelled wife for a while, the ridiculous idea came to him – as a combination of abstraction and words – that he and his wife would never have children now, not only because she was dead, but because her ovaries and uterus had been ingested by the naked woman, and that was a fact which could never change.

And he realized this, too: he realized that he had never been hungrier.

'My mother,' Erthmun declared – he was still holding Marty bent backward over one of his stoves – 'writes poetry! Isn't that civilized? What more civilized thing is there than fucking poetry?'

'Uhn—' Marty groaned.

'It's very bad poetry,' Erthmun said. 'But still it's civilized because *she* is civilized. My mother is a very civilized woman. And because *she's* civilized, so am I!'

'Yes,' Marty managed.

'But poets can kill, and have,' Erthmun declared. 'Poets bring us more pain than whole armies of armed men, I think!'

Marty said nothing.

'I'm not a poet,' Erthmun said. His tone had softened. He spoke in what could almost pass for a quiet and conversational tone, now, except that there was tension in it. 'I'm a cop. I investigate murder. That is what I do and it is what society expects of me, so I do it happily, and well. I get money for it, and a place to live. I write nothing, I create nothing. And I have never killed.' He paused, cocked his head, continued, 'Perhaps I should begin. I think there's something very deep inside me that wants me to begin killing. It feels deprived, neglected, left out . . . of the human experience. Do you have that same feeling – ' short pause ' – Marty?'

'No,' said Marty.

'I think you do. I think you may be lying.'

'No,' said Marty.

Erthmun felt terror, panic, desperation. He could see a life in it, and pain – Marty's life, and Marty's pain. It made him soften his grip on the man's shirt collar. Marty stayed put. The terror, panic and desperation passed. Erthmun's grip strengthened again, and he said, 'You're talking to me, aren't you, my friend?'

'No,' said Marty.

'But you are. You're telling me all about yourself. You're telling me you want to live and you're telling me about your children. You're telling me that you don't want me to hurt you, and you're telling me that you don't like pain. Shit, that's nothing new. Who likes pain?'

'I'm saying nothing,' said Marty.

'I can *hear* it, my friend. I can hear you speak.'

'No,' said Marty.

'And the big question is – am I going to listen?'

*

Greta loved chocolate. Not cheap chocolate. Not mud.
Expensive chocolate, chocolate made with pleasure
and with pleasure in mind. Chocolate was childhood.
Childhood was life.

And what did these people here, in this city, know
of pleasure? They took no pleasure in anything, they
moved about from sunset to dawn to dawn to sunset,
and their weeks became years, and their years were
done.

Hers were just beginning.

Forty

Summer, outside the house on Four Mile Creek
The man asked, 'Is it salvageable, do you think?' His own guess was no. The paint had long since flaked off the clapboards, the grouting had crumbled from much of the stone foundation, the chimneys were little more than stumps.

The real estate agent was a woman who was new to the area, but she wasn't new to real estate, or to architecture and construction, and she said, 'I think it is. It's a beautiful house underneath that dark patina of age.'

The man looked at her and smiled. 'You're something of a poet, aren't you?'

She blushed. She didn't know what to say. She had seen her phrase merely as a descriptive enticement, although it was true enough as well – the house was certainly salvageable. She explained, 'All the windows are intact, as remarkable as that may seem. Some of them are cracked, certainly, but they can be repaired. And since the windows are intact, and the roof itself is not too far gone, then the house hasn't been victimized by the elements in the way that it might otherwise have been.'

'Even though it's been empty for how long? Thirty-five years?'

'Yes. About that long.'

They were standing just outside the house's grey, stylized picket fence – much of the fence had fallen and only a few tilting sections remained – and the man said, 'This is very pretty. It looks hand-built.'

The real estate agent nodded. 'It is.'

'What a pity that it can't be salvaged as well.' Short pause. 'Could we look inside?'

'Of course.'

PARTIAL TRANSCRIPT OF THE INITIAL INTERROGATION OF ROBERT W. GARNISH, AS CONDUCTED BY DETECTIVE PAUL MCBRIDE OF THE 20TH PRECINCT

P.M.: This won't wash, and you know it, Robert. This is crap from the get-go.

R.G.: Don't call me Robert. My name's not Robert. It's Bob.

P.M.: Okay, Bob. Your call.

R.G.: Shit, too.

P.M.: Yes, you're right, Bob. It's not your call. It's our call. And I'd say our call is for twenty-five to life.

Shit, Bob, if it were up to me I'd feed you to the
fucking bears at the fucking Central Park zoo. That
would be a fitting punishment. That would be . . .
shit, that would be fucking *irony*, Bob. But it's not up
to me, and you can thank your lucky stars for that.

R.G.: I don't have any.

P.M.: Any what, Bob?

R.G.: Lucky stars.

P.M.: Damn right, Bob. All the fucking stars in the
sky and not a lucky one for you. You've had a
fucking tough few months, haven't you, Bob? No
job, no place to live, nothing to fucking *eat*!

R.G.: Yeah.

P.M.: Sure, you have. We've all had a tough time.
Life's tough. Living's tough. Finding enough to
fucking *eat* is tough, isn't it?

R.G.: I didn't do that to her. I told you who did it,
and it wasn't me.

P.M.: Yes, you did, Bob. And the amazing thing
is this: the amazing thing is – you actually expect
us to fucking believe that fantasy. Naked woman, my
ass!

R.G.: It happened.

P.M.: No, it didn't. We both know what
happened. We both know what happened. So tell
me, Bob – how was it? Was it finger-licking good
stuff? Did it go down good? Was it *nourishing*,
Robert? Did it contain your daily allowance of
vitamins and fucking minerals?

R.G.: Shit on you!

P.M.: Tell me something, Bob: How do you feel about chocolate?

Two miles from the house on Four Mile Creek

What had he expected? Had he expected to find her here? Had he expected to see her sitting by this stream and spooning mud into her doll's mouth? That was the past. That was thirty years ago or more. She had been a child, then, and so had he.

He turned his head. He was in a valley, and the tall golden grasses were swaying in a soft breeze. The white noise they created was comforting, and called up memories that he had long suppressed. He thought that, from this vantage point, he could see the house. But he could not. It was too far away, over the hillock. He would have to do a lot of walking and climbing if he wanted to see it.

He looked at the little stream again. If there were ghosts, would she be sitting there, doing what she had been doing so long ago? Perhaps. If so, he did not have the power to see her.

Why had he come back here? he wondered. The answer was obvious. He had come back because this was where he had begun his life. There was something sacred in that. Childhood itself was sacred. Adulthood wasn't. Adulthood was profane, violent and perverse. But he was trapped in it. There was no way around it. He was trapped in it and he had to make the most of it.

He climbed the hill that was on the opposite side of the stream, and went back to his rented car. He sat in the car for a long while and asked himself if, after driving all this way, he was really going to simply turn around and go back to his city without visiting the house he had grown up in. Yes, he realized. That was what he was going to do. The house itself meant nothing. The house was simply a dark blotch on the tall, golden grasses. It was wood, shingles, cement, stone and memories that were not as delicious as he had once thought.

And he had work to do.

He started the car and drove off.

They were on the second floor of the house on Four Mile Creek and the man lifted his foot and brought it down hard on the wood floor. 'Solid enough,' he said.

'It is,' agreed the real estate agent.

They were near a window. It looked out, through the sad remains of a lace curtain, on hills and fields lush with golden grasses that were swaying gracefully in a playful breeze. The man stepped over to the window, pushed aside the curtain, looked out at the golden grasses. 'This is beautiful,' he said. 'Very beautiful.'

'Best place on earth,' said the real estate agent. 'A great place to raise kids.'

'I would say, though,' noted the man, 'that it's hell in winter.'

'Before the bond issue was put through,' explained

the real estate agent, 'I would not have recommended that anyone live here in the winter. But, as you know, there is a road being built to take the place of the one we drove on to get here.'

'Uh-huh,' said the man. He seemed suddenly distracted. He glanced back at her, said, 'I see some dust rising at the horizon. What do you think it is?'

She came over to the window, looked out. 'It's that dirt road. When it's dry like it's been, cars can kick up a hell of a lot of dust on it.'

'Yeah,' he said. 'I see.' He paused, continued, 'And what do you think that is?' He pointed to indicate an area a hundred yards from the house.

She looked, said, 'An animal.'

'What animal?'

'Take your pick.'

'Yes,' he said. 'I see now. It's a raccoon.' He paused, continued, 'I thought they were nocturnal.'

'Yes, well they usually are,' said the real estate agent with an odd tone of apology.

'Then what's that one doing out in daylight?'

The real estate agent hesitated, then said, 'I would caution you about some of the wildlife.'

CRITICAL WAVE

THE EUROPEAN SCIENCE FICTION & FANTASY REVIEW

"CRITICAL WAVE is the most consistently interesting and intelligent review on the sf scene."
- Michael Moorcock.

"One of the best of the business journals...
I never miss a copy..." - Bruce Sterling.

"Intelligent and informative, one of my key sources of news, reviews and comments." - Stephen Baxter.

"I don't feel informed until I've read it."
- Ramsey Campbell.

"Don't waver - get WAVE!" - Brian W Aldiss.

CRITICAL WAVE is published six times per year and has established a reputation for hard-hitting news coverage, perceptive essays on the state of the genre and incisive reviews of the latest books, comics and movies. Regular features include publishing news, portfolios by Europe's leading sf and fantasy artists, extensive club, comic mart and convention listings, interviews with prominent authors and editors, fiction market reports, fanzine and magazine reviews and convention reports.

Previous contributors have included: MICHAEL MOORCOCK, IAIN BANKS, CLIVE BARKER, LISA TUTTLE, BOB SHAW, COLIN GREENLAND, DAVID LANGFORD, ROBERT HOLDSTOCK, GARRY KILWORTH, SHAUN HUTSON, DAVID WINGROVE, TERRY PRATCHETT, RAMSEY CAMPBELL, LARRY NIVEN, BRIAN W ALDISS, ANNE GAY, STEPHEN BAXTER, RAYMOND FEIST, CHRIS CLAREMONT and STORM CONSTANTINE.

A six issue subscription costs only eight pounds and fifty pence or a sample copy one pound and ninety-five pence; these rates only apply to the UK, overseas readers should contact the address below for further details. Cheques or postal orders should be made payable to "Critical Wave Publications" and sent to: M Tudor, 845 Alum Rock Road, Birmingham, B8 2AG. Please allow 30 days for delivery.

Also available in Gollancz Horror

Price correct at time of going to press (August 1995)

The Torturer

JIM BALLANTYNE

A razorblade ride to the edge of the abyss . . .

Matt Trace takes pride in his work. Unique in the criminal underworld, he is a new kind of hitman. Not a crude thug, but a skilled, detached craftsman in the art of pain – a violence designer. For a price, a very handsome price, he can be hired – he will torture your enemies and send you back the evidence on videotape.

But Matt Trace has enemies of his own – and not just those compiling a dossier on him in the police department. For in the course of his exceptional career, he has made a deadly mistake. And soon he must deal with another, more terrifying kind of underworld altogether.

£4.99   0 575 05228 7

Nocturne

MARK CHADBOURN

He woke up on a New Orleans street car. He was wearing his best suit and carrying a walletful of travellers' cheques, a reservation at a smart hotel and a suitcase of bloodstained clothes.

But David Easter had no idea how he got there. The last thing he remembered, he was working in a south London record shop.

Somewhere in the city is a girl who holds the key to what has happened to him. As David sets out to find her he is drawn inexorably into a darkness that stretches back to the dawn of the jazz age – and now threatens not only David but the city itself . . .

Nocturne. A superbly atmospheric novel of terror.

£5.99   0 575 05793 9

Archangel

GARRY D. KILWORTH

In 1997 an angel fell to earth – but now the stakes
have risen . . .

There's a demon abroad in London, a soul so
corrupt and foul that Satan himself has recruited
him from the legions of the dead. Only one entity
in Heaven can counter his power – an Archangel,
one of the eighth order of the celestial hierarchy.

Rocketing into the city comes the most
awesome power ever seen by human eyes – blazing
with Divine light and as volatile as a nuclear
bomb.

Humanity must suffer as their battle rages. And
then the Thames starts turning to blood . . .

£5.99   0 575 05768 8

Also in VG Horror by Garry D. Kilworth

Angel

'Gore-on-the-floor horror, with an urban cop twist
. . . high quality creepiness and more ideas than a
dozen other horrors' Kim Newman

£4.99   0 575 05721 1